A Kind of Redemption

Stories by

Stephen Hathaway

A
Kind
of
Redemption

1991

Louisiana State University Press
Baton Rouge and London

Designer: Amanda McDonald Key
Typeface: Trump Mediaeval
Typesetter: G & S Typesetters, Inc.
Printer and binder: Thomson-Shore, Inc.

Library of Congress Cataloging-in-Publication Data

Hathaway, Stephen, 1945–
   A kind of redemption : stories / by Stephen Hathaway.
     p.   cm.
   ISBN 0-8071-1611-4 (cloth)
   I. Title.
   PS3558.A748K56   1991
813'.54—dc20   90-49920
                                                                     CIP

The author offers grateful acknowledgment to the editors of the following
publications, in which some of these stories first appeared: *American Institute of Discussion: Accent on Fiction,* IV (1989); *American Institute of
Discussion Review,* I (Winter, 1985); *Itinerary Four: Fiction* (1977); *Quarterly West* (Autumn, 1978). "A Kind of Redemption" was first published in
Kansas Quarterly, XV (Spring, 1983).

The author thanks the National Endowment for the Arts for a Creative Writing Fellowship Grant, which allowed him to live in Cambridge, England,
where portions of the manuscript were written in 1982. The author also
thanks James Lee Burke, Frances Majors, Bryan Hay, and Aaron Van Deusen
for their friendship and support during the preparation of the manuscript.

Publication of this book has been supported by a grant from the National
Endowment for the Arts in Washington, D.C., a federal agency.

For my daughter Margaret

And to the memory of her grandfather
Willis Hathaway,
Master Sergeant, United States Army Air Corps,
1934–1945

He knew that the essence of war is violence,
and that moderation in war is imbecility.
                    —Thomas Babington Macaulay

Contents

A Kind of Redemption

WHADDYA mean, you ain't going to Viet Nam?" the old man says, making Nam rhyme with Sam, when Sharpe calls with the news.

"There's something in my blood. I got it from you from when you were sick in the Philippines."

"Well, I'll be a son of a bitch," Sharpe's father mutters into the telephone. Ralph Sharpe was on Corregidor, survived the Death March, malaria, round worms, dysentery. He was shipped home as soon as he was well enough to travel after liberation, and his son was born nine months later.

"Eighteen months in California," Sharpe says. "What luck."

"And all them guys over there," the old man says.

Sharpe can sense an argument brewing. "Look, Pop, there's a long line of guys waiting to use the phone. I better go."

"I'll tell your mother you called."

"Thanks, Pop. Bye."

Three days ago, Sharpe stood in line at the Overseas Replacement Station with the other clerks from his class while the clerks behind the long gray counters reviewed their files. "More hassles, more bullshit," he grumbled when the specialist told him to report to the medical station a half mile's walk in a cold, early morning drizzle. After his orders for Viet Nam were canceled, Sharpe returned to the processing station to thank his benefactor, Specialist Higgins, who introduced him to Sergeant Banquo, who said he'd get Sharpe assigned to his section. Now, his future brighter

than it has been for the past six months, Sharpe takes
the bus into Monterey to treat himself to dinner on the
wharf.

Orientals are all the same to Sharpe's father. If it wasn't
the Japanese, it was the Koreans; if not the Koreans,
then the Chinese. And now there are Vietnamese, Cam-
bodians, Thais. "They're all gooks," Sharpe's father
will say. Sharpe has heard the stories so many times
that they blend into one, a mélange of brutality and
degradation, snakes, maggots, misery and death. The
old man used to take him to the VFW bar to hear other
litanies of humiliation and terror, bayonets, behead-
ings, and always, Bataan. It all came together in the
Death March, and Sharpe's father would take over, de-
scribing the shame of the American Army.

Crazy with hunger and thirst, they were driven the
length of the Bataan Peninsula. If a man fell out of line,
a Japanese soldier would shoot or bayonet him. A corporal lying on his back was shot in the face two yards
from Sharpe's father. When the men around him began
yelling, he shouted at them to shut up and hold their
ranks or they'd all be killed.

A man tripped and Sharpe's father caught him and
held him up. The man said he wanted to die and
Sharpe's father told him he would die pretty soon if he
wasn't careful. A guard with a sword watched them,
then moved up the line. They got the man to camp,
but he died anyway.

They boarded trains at San Fernando, crammed into
freight cars so tightly that they couldn't move. When
the train stopped, they were ordered out of the cars and
started walking again to Camp O'Donnell. The Japanese didn't have any food for them and they were taken
into a clearing and beaten with clubs and rifle butts.
Some of the Japanese officers tried to make their men
stop, but it didn't do any good. The only thing that
kept them alive, Sharpe's father said, was their hatred
of the Japanese.

His father would continue, telling about camp life

and how they cadged food from the guards and natives, treated disease, buried their dead, while Sharpe stared at their reflections in the mirror behind the bar, unable to comprehend their anger over something that happened so long ago. Week after week they told the same old stories, voices rising with the accumulation of memory and empty bottles. After a while, cheap whiskey and war stories ceased to interest him, and Sharpe made excuses to avoid going there with his father.

His father wanted him to apply to West Point, and he did, but was turned down. He studied history instead. He took a course in Oriental philosophy and the arguments with his father grew intense. "Whaddya know from books?" his father would say. "I was there, goddamit, I was there. Don't tell me from books." When Sharpe tried to explain what he was learning in college, his father would say, "I know what I know," and that was the end of it.

When he knew he would be drafted, Sharpe considered going to Canada to escape, but didn't, half afraid his father would come after him. The old man saw him off at the bus station, his face softening when they shook hands and said good-bye. "I was there," his father said quietly. "Good luck." Sharpe boarded the bus with the eighteen- and nineteen-year-olds, feeling ancient and out of shape at twenty-three.

He'd done all right, in spite of the age difference, and was promoted at the end of basic training. There were times, especially when they were marching in the mornings, when Sharpe would gaze ahead at the double column of men, rifles over their shoulders and dust rising around their boots, and feel a sense of belonging, almost pride. He imagined them marching to relieve Bastogne, equipment clanging softly as they tramped through a snowy winter night. He never thought of going to Viet Nam. When he received orders assigning him to Fort Ord, he called his father.

"Infantry?" his father said.

"Personnel."

"Did you volunteer for that?"

"I'm not volunteering for anything. They can draft me and do what they want with me, but I'm not going to volunteer for it."

"I never had no damn U.S. in front of my serial number. We all went Regular Army."

"It was different then," Sharpe said.

At the restaurant, the waitress brings him a cup of clam chowder and he orders a bourbon and soda. The bay is calm, disturbed only by occasional ground swells that cause the water to rise against the boulders and pilings along shore. He finishes the soup and lights a cigarette, sipping his drink while he waits for his lobster. They can have two years of his life, but that's all. Then he's going to graduate school. He will use the GI Bill and take every penny that he's entitled to. When he thought he was going to Viet Nam, he accepted his fate. Now that he's not going, he accepts that, too. He knows that he has been spared because of his father's suffering, also that there is no acceptable way to express this to the old man. His lobster and half bottle of chablis arrive. He picks at his food with the special fork, gazing from time to time at the bay as the tide begins to come in.

Every man working at the Overseas Replacement Station has gotten his job in the same way, snatched from the war at the last minute. Sergeant Banquo's wife tried to commit suicide. Higgins' father died. Mead, the financial records specialist, has a brother in the 1st Cav. The men whose records they process aren't as lucky.

Sharpe's job is to stand behind a counter and check their 201 Files to make sure they have been properly trained for overseas duty. He then asks each man, "Has any member of your family been killed, captured, or wounded in a combat situation while serving on active duty with a United States military unit in the Republic of Viet Nam?" After the first day, the words run together into a single phrase, like a priest mumbling at mass. This is their last chance to get out of it. If a man answers yes, his orders will be canceled and he'll be reassigned to serve out his time at a stateside post. But the men always say no, and Sharpe hands them their files and sends them on their way.

It gets to the point that he can tell when an infantry company is coming, even before they reach the crest of the hill fifty yards from the building. They march sullenly, the sergeants barking out the cadences in the damp California air. They get sick a lot during training and are confined to their company areas to protect the rest of the post. For identification they have white canvas strips sewn over their shirt pockets so that if one of them leaves his company area, he can be spotted by the MPs and returned to his unit for punishment. They sit on benches outside the processing station, smoking and coughing and blowing their noses while their sergeants yell at them and get them ready.

They are younger than Sharpe expected, like kids dressed up in Army suits as they stand in line, red-eyed and sniffling, waiting impatiently to have their records checked one last time so they can draw their pay and take thirty days' leave before reporting for overseas shipment. While at home they're supposed to get over their colds so they'll be healthy when they get to Viet Nam.

He feels uncomfortable around them, grateful that they have to form their line fifteen feet from his counter. He watches their faces, wondering which will be wounded, which will die, take drugs, be scarred for life. Higgins and the others openly harass them. Each man carries his own files but isn't supposed to tamper with them. If a man drops his records, a voice rings out:

"Hey, You!"

"Yes, Sir."

"Pick that shit up and get over here. Right now! I told you not to fuck around with your files. Gimme those things and get your ass into the latrine and start cleaning. You're last in line."

When the man leaves, Higgins warns the others.

"Straighten up that line. Don't fuck with your records or you'll wind up in the latrine with that other guy."

The men do as they are told. Without their sergeants, who wait outside or drink coffee with Sergeant Banquo, they obey the orders of anybody who shouts at them. Sharpe stops noticing individual faces as they process 300 or 400 a day. They process 550 men for shipment to Viet Nam the first time Sharpe sends somebody to the latrine.

"Damn it," he says. "We told you not to fool around with your records. Give me those files and go into the latrine."

"Not bad," Higgins says when the man is gone, "but you gotta put more heart into it. Belt it out like you're used to giving orders. These guys are grunts; they're used to getting shit on."

"They're just kids," Sharpe says.

"Kids, schmids. They'll be all right. Just do your job and don't think about them."

"I'm going to try to get out early," Sharpe tells his father. "I've been accepted at graduate school and I want to start in the fall."

"*Graduate school?*" the old man says. "Jesus Christ, I don't understand you. There's a war going on—don't you understand that?"

"I'm not in the war. All I do is shuffle papers."

"If you're not there to shuffle papers, somebody else has to do it."

"Pop, it's different now. It doesn't work that way anymore."

"Nobody talked like that after Pearl Harbor. You can't win a war if everybody doesn't do his share. Graduate school. What the hell's going on in this country?"

"My brother."

"What's that?" Sharpe looks up at the skinny black kid.

"My brother. Sniper got 'em."

Sharpe glances at the file in front of him. Jiggets, Tyrone. PFC. Regular Army, Enlisted. Infantry. Just like the old man.

"When?"

"Sixty-four. In the Delta."

Sharpe calculates that Tyrone was thirteen in 1964. He smiles. "Tyrone, this is your lucky day. We can get your orders changed so you won't have to go to Viet Nam." He studies the boy's face for a sign of comprehension. Tyrone shakes his head.

"Don't you understand? You don't have to go."

Tyrone scowls. "I'm goin'," he says.

Sharpe waves for Sergeant Banquo to come over. "It's crazy over there," he says. "You don't want to go to Viet Nam."

"What's going on here?" Sergeant Banquo says.

"His brother was killed in sixty-four. I told him he didn't have to go, but he says he's going anyway."

"Don't be a fool, kid," Banquo says.

"They got my brother."

"So what're you gonna do? Find the guy that did it? That's a shitty idea, kid."

"I'll get some of them."

"That's bullshit," Banquo says. "That's World War II talk. It's a different ball game now."

"There's nothin' that says I can't go, is there?"

"Nobody can stop you."

"Then I'm goin'."

Before allowing Tyrone to leave, Sergeant Banquo makes him sign a waiver.

"Nigger's gonna get his shit blown away," Banquo says when Tyrone is gone.

Tonight, Sharpe has gone to the wharf again for dinner, ordering swordfish and a bottle of champagne. He finishes his meal and dawdles over the champagne, sipping it slowly while the sun sets and the bay grows dark, until the waitress tells him he will have to leave because they need his table for other customers. He still has a third of the bottle of champagne, and she gives him a paper sack so he can take it with him. Knowing she won't expect it, he leaves three dollars on the table for her.

It is warm as he wanders along the wharf, pausing to look in shop windows and read menus at restaurants. The air smells of creosote and cooking grease and fish. He moves through the milling crowds of tourists and soldiers, his champagne bottle tucked under his arm, then heads for the end of the wharf, where it is dark, and sits on a bench by some pilings. Breakers are crashing six hundred yards out, illuminated by an almost-full moon. He drinks from the bottle, crushing the sack around the neck as he raises it.

Another infantry company is due tomorrow. They will join the others Sharpe has processed and some will be wounded and some will die. He tries to figure out how many men he's sent to Viet Nam, but gives up. He knows it is thousands, and that there will be thousands more before the Army releases him. When they return from the war they will have stories. They will grow middle-aged and flabby and sit in bars as his father does and recount what they saw and did. Sharpe drinks from the bottle. Tyrone, too, will have his war and, if he survives, his stories. Fuck Tyrone. Sharpe offered him a chance for life and he rejected it. If he gets shot, it will be his own fault.

The others don't have a choice. They stand in line with those stupid canvas stripes over their pockets, waiting to be sent to war. All they'll have when it's over will be a handful of medals and their memories. He thinks of the men at the VFW bar, still bitter and raging after twenty-five years. At least they can take some pride in what they did. But these guys in Viet Nam, what will they be like, Sharpe wonders.

A family of tourists separates from the crowds and heads for the end of the wharf, probably to look at the waves. He drinks from his bottle and stares at them. He will stand his ground. They can go someplace else if they want to look at the ocean.

He is beginning to understand something about his father. The old man has done something that Sharpe will never do and there is no way for Sharpe to know what his father knows. He can read books and try to imagine it, but he can never really know it for himself. It is his father's, not his. He thinks of his father and the man who wanted to die during the Death March, and can almost hear the old man's voice: "I was there, goddamit, I was there." Sharpe feels a sudden sense of wonder.

The wind has picked up and the waves crash higher and harder against the pilings. If he stays much longer he'll get wet. Already, his clothes are damp from the salt spray. Beyond the breakers and the bay is the ocean and Corregidor and Bataan, and beyond that is the South China Sea and Viet Nam. He takes a drink and looks toward the ocean and the two wars, trying to imagine the things his father knows; failing, he feels a sense of loss.

He will withdraw his application to get out early, he decides. Graduate school can wait for a semester. The least he can do is serve out his time. He owes it to the old man.

"What's that, Daddy?" The tourist family has stopped twenty-five feet from the end of the wharf; the youngest child points at him.

"Just a GI," the father says. "It's nothing to worry about."

What the hell, Sharpe thinks. He stands and pours the rest of the champagne into the water, then deposits the bottle in a trash barrel and heads back toward the crowds, vacating his spot so the kids can look at the ocean.

Pringle's Moratorium

THE six Vietnamese translators who arrived without fanfare at Fort Ord, California, in February of 1970 made the naturally suspicious Specialist Five Lew Pringle more than a little uneasy. Ensconced behind his desk in the post's personnel office, the men's 201 Files spread in an arc before him, he brooded over the same cryptic notation that appeared in each one: "NO ASG IN MI OR ASA— AUTH AR 614-200." No assignments in Military Intelligence or Army Security Agency. What could it mean? Lighting a cigarette from the one he'd just finished, he struggled to ferret out the pattern that would explain the presence of the men on his post.

All six were college graduates and had been drafted between April Fools' Day and the middle of May, 1969. (Pringle, a Dartmouth graduate, had been drafted April 30 of the same year.) Two, Specialists Doyle and Sharkey, had master's degrees, in linguistics and forest management, respectively. The others, Specialists Breslin, Dent, Graber, and Grote, all had some graduate training. Their average age was twenty-four years, seven months, and their average IQ was just under 130. After basic training, they'd been sent to Fort Bliss, Texas, for nine months of intensive training in Vietnamese, achieving rudimentary diplomatic fluency and promotion to the rank of Specialist Four. Then they'd been packed off to Fort Ord.

Specialist Pringle smelled a rat.

He dialed the number for C Company and asked for Captain Archer, the earnest young incompetent who was afraid of him. "Archie, it's me, Lew. Whaddya make of these new guys who speak Vietnamese?"

"Their orders say TDY till they pass the personnel course, then we ship 'em to Nam."

"Unh-unh. *We* can't ship them anywhere; they're under Pentagon control."

"So?"

"It seems odd. What if these guys aren't who they say they are?"

Captain Archer didn't reply.

"These are high-dollar guys, Archie. Why send them to a dump like this and stick them in *your* company where all they can do is learn how to shuffle papers? Something's fishy."

Lowering his voice, Specialist Pringle unfolded his hypothesis to the anxious Captain Archer: the six weren't really Vietnamese translators at all. It was a ruse and those entries in their files about no assignments in Army Security were phony. Instead, they were an investigative team that had been sent to dig up dirt in time for the upcoming general inspection, and if they weren't careful Captain Archer would be S.O.L.

"Believe me, Archie, these guys play hardball. Here's what: send them over here one at a time and I'll find out what they're up to. Start with Grote. He's got orders in his file making him Acting Sergeant. Probably fake, but he's the likely team leader. I tell you, Archie, this isn't something to fool around with."

Captain Archer exhaled a long breath. "Whatever you say, Lew."

Formerly Acting Sergeant, now Specialist Four, Timothy Grote was mopping the mess hall floor as punishment for refusing to do push-ups when Sergeant Crabbe suddenly appeared and told him to get his ass over to Personnel because Specialist Pringle wanted to see him. Right away. Grote unrolled his sleeves, retrieved his shabby copy of *Moby Dick*, and started for the door before thinking to ask where Personnel was.

"Quarter mile up that road there, then left. Get a move on."

Before being drafted, Timothy Grote had spent five months in the West Indies with the Peace Corps, until he was kicked out for insubordination and generally being a pain in the neck. While still in the Reception Station at Fort Knox, he'd been interviewed by a Lieutenant Kalodny, who told him his score on the Army Language Aptitude Test (ALAT) was exceptional ("the highest I've ever seen") and that he'd make "a darned good candidate for the Defense Language Institute at Fort Bliss." From DLI, he'd proceed to the intelligence school at Fort Meade for further training as an interrogator. In Viet Nam, he'd probably be assigned to a division-level intelligence unit, where he might be obliged to make occasional forays "into the field," which sounded ominous. On the other hand, Lieutenant Kalodny concluded, "the war might well be over by the time you finish your language course." That cinched it.

When he arrived at Fort Bliss, Grote was ordered to report to Biggs Field, a detached World War II–vintage airfield, little used except for the mysterious comings and goings of unmarked aircraft practicing for secret missions in the Middle East. Biggs Field, he and his colleagues were told, was off limits to Fort Bliss and vice versa. Thereafter, they never set foot on Fort Bliss again, except once in November when they were bused over to have their teeth cleaned.

"Your mission is to learn Vietnamese, and nothing else," amiable Captain Digby told them at their orientation. "When you leave here, you will know the language so well that you will *dream* in Vietnamese. We will do everything possible to assist you." He ended his chat on a menacing note, however. "Your instructors are Vietnamese nationals; under *no* circumstance are you to allow photographs to be taken of you. If your pictures turn up in Viet Nam, you could be in world of shit. It's happened before."

Instead of the raucous barracks they'd been forced to endure in basic training, they were assigned rooms in a former officers' dormitory. Instead of the twelve-to sixteen-hour-a-day grind of their first eight weeks in uniform, they attended class six hours a day, then retired to the library or their rooms to prepare for the following day's lessons. Instead of the dreary tedium of KP and constant inspections, the mess hall was staffed by civilians and, for a nominal fee, the men could hire Mexican women to ineffectually dust and mop their rooms. Most astonishing of all, Timothy Grote, so ignominiously booted out of the Peace Corps, was appointed Acting Sergeant and made class leader.

If he was tolerated by the twenty men in his charge, it was not for any essential leadership qualities he possessed. Rather, it was because he grasped that they'd learn better if they were left alone. To flunk out of DLI meant Fort Polk, Louisiana, and infantry training, which could lead to a sad end in a snake- and leech-infested rice paddy. So they studied their Vietnamese diligently, playing for time in the vain hope that the war would end before it was their turn to go. Acting Sergeant Grote's job was to represent their interests to Captain Digby and take the heat when they misbehaved.

If he was admired at all by his men, it was for his memorable performances on their rare visits to the parade ground. To Grote, close-order drill was a nightmare abstraction of commands and countercommands that signified nothing and led to no satisfactory conclusion. The men (Grote suspected them of being deliberately inept) would end up facing every which way, crash into each other and fall down, and indulge themselves in unsoldierly giggling. Once, surveying the chaos wrought by his bewildering commands, he suddenly shouted, "HALT! Everybody . . . norrth . . . FACE!" When he'd gotten them into what vaguely resembled a formation, he told them they were a disgrace, then sent them back to their rooms to do their homework.

This prima donna life ended when they took their final examinations and it was time to move on to Fort Meade for interrogator training. It was then that it was discovered that a mistake had been made: six of the men were ineligible and would have to be trained elsewhere to perform different duties. Breslin, Grote, and Sharkey were barred because of Peace Corps service. ("The Peace Corps doesn't hire spooks and MI doesn't trust the Peace Corps," Captain Digby chuckled.) Fabian Dent, a thorn in Grote's side throughout their language training, was the son of a State Department official in Upper Volta. ("Can't compromise the Agency," Digby said laconically.) Doyle's and Graber's security clearances hadn't panned out. ("How those dickheads ever got in is a mystery to me," Digby grumbled.) In truth, these facts had been known all along, but it was in the interest of the Defense Language Institute, a prestigious and profitable enterprise, to produce graduates, and so they'd been disregarded.

Specialist Grote, who'd become friendly with Captain Digby, was aware of all this. Specialist Pringle, trapped in the darkness of his suspicions, was not.

Specialist Pringle was pretending to be absorbed in Grote's file and gestured for him to sit. "Mind if I call you Tim?"

Grote shook his head. "What's up?"

"Nothing, really, Tim. It's just that we don't see guys like you very often and we like to know what you're up to."

Grote stared blankly at him, and Pringle, spotting Grote's book, decided to change his tack. "Ah!" he exclaimed, "*Moby Dick.* I did my senior thesis on it at Dartmouth. Fascinating guy . . . really fascinating."

"My last seminar at Michigan State was on Melville," Grote responded cheerfully. "My professor was David Mead; perhaps you've heard of him?"

"Meade? I don't recall a Meade right now," Pringle said, momentarily alarmed by the reference. Christ, these guys are slick, he thought.

"One of the great teachers," Grote replied, momentarily indulging himself in an academic reverie.

What's he getting at? Pringle wondered. "Well, Tim," he said affably, "How long you reckon you'll be with us?"

Again, the blank stare. "Till we get our orders for Viet Nam."

An idea was vaguely formulating itself in Pringle's mind, an idea so preposterous and subversive that his own impulsiveness shocked him.

"You know," he said conspiratorily, "you're under Pentagon control, and even though we can't move you, you'll have to go sometime."

Grote nodded warily.

"And because of the time difference I've only got three hours a day when I can talk to them. Here's what: as long as they don't tell me to ship you guys out, I won't ask."

Grasping the implications of Pringle's offer, Grote said quietly, "That's really decent of you."

"Nothing illegal," Pringle added hastily.

"Of course," Grote replied.

When Grote had left, Pringle sat at his desk, chain-smoking and marveling at what he'd proposed. Something in Grote's manner convinced him that they weren't spooks but just poor slobs like himself who were unlucky enough to get themselves drafted. It wouldn't make any difference whether they went to Viet Nam or not. Besides, who knew what might happen to them if they went over there?

"We're going to have to baby Pringle," Grote told the others over beer and pizza that night. "I don't know what the hell's going on, but I think he's going to help us."

"Help us what?" Fabian Dent demanded.

"I don't know about you, but *I'm* in no hurry to go to Viet Nam. If we can last a month here, every day after that is one we won't have to spend over there."

Grote was right. After another month, they'd have thirteen remaining in order to fulfill their two-year obligations, and Army regulations required that they be given thirty days' leave before they could be sent overseas. Hence, every day after thirty that they spent in California would be doubly sweet. They agreed to cooperate with Specialist Pringle.

"He's a nervous guy," Grote concluded. "Let's be nice to him."

Pringle would have to persuade Captain Archer and Sergeant Crabbe that it would be in their interests to keep the translators around.

"I couldn't get much out of Grote," Pringle told them in a confidential tone that same night at the NCO club, "except that slip he made by the reference to Fort Meade. We can't let these guys out of our sight until the IG inspection is over."

They decided to find jobs on the post for the translators after they completed their personnel courses. Jobs in conspicuous places where they could be watched. Meanwhile, Pringle would interview the others to see if he could trick them into revealing more than Grote had. It would be a delicate operation, but Pringle was confident that Captain Archer's ragtag company would weather the storm.

"Whoever heard of Vietnamese-speaking personnel specialists?" Pringle scoffed. "Don't worry, Archie, we've got this thing under control."

The translators were quick learners and mastered their two clerking courses in under two weeks, whereas ordinary soldiers had been known to take as long as sixteen. Pringle entered their new Military Occupational Specialties in their 201 Files: 71H2L94 (Personnel Specialist; Two Languages; Vietnamese, Saigon Dialect). Then he went to work finding jobs for them.

It would probably be best to keep them in pairs. Doyle and Dent would go to Finance, Breslin and Graber to Medical Records. Grote and Sharkey he sent to the Overseas Replacement Station, where they'd be under the tutelage of Staff Sergeant Dreyfuss, a Pringle crony. Had he telephoned the Pentagon as he was supposed to, the six translators would have been off the post and on their way to Viet Nam three days after taking the clerk final examination.

"Everything's in place," he told Archer. "Now all we have to do is keep them under surveillance and wait."

"I've gotta hand it to you, Lew," Archer said. "This is working out better than I thought."

Next, Pringle phoned Staff Sergeant Dreyfuss, who'd quickly come to appreciate the translators for what they were worth. "They're fast and they're efficient," he bubbled, "and they don't fuck things up. I wish we had more guys like this."

"Yeah," Pringle said, smiling inwardly, "they're a real windfall."

Dreyfuss' good opinion of the translators was echoed by the section chiefs in Finance and Medical Records. Pringle's social capital was rising, an unexpected boon. Maybe, he thought, Washington will forget about them altogether and they won't have to go to Viet Nam at all.

For their part, the translators knew Pringle had done them a favor, but they didn't know why. It didn't really matter—as long as they were working at Fort Ord, they weren't in Viet Nam. Responding to a newspaper ad, Grote and Dent discovered a decrepit motel in Pacific Grove that had adjoining suites, complete with showers and a shared kitchen. The six pooled their money to pay for a month in advance, turned in their bedding to the Quartermaster, and moved off post into the motel, a quarter mile from the ocean. They celebrated their thirty-day milestone with a tub of spaghetti and two gallons of throat-scraping California burgundy.

Hypothesizing that their reprieve had something to do with their previous status as apprentice interrogators, they upped the ante by having their former colleagues from Fort Bliss send letters on Fort Meade stationery, whose arrival was noted by Sergeant Crabbe and reported to Specialist Pringle. ("What do you bet they're written in code?" Pringle asked the befuddled Archer, who was beginning to have doubts about Pringle's spy theory.)

The translators worked from 7:30 until 4:30, with an hour off for lunch in the mess hall. At the end of the work day, having no place on the post to call home, they hung around the library or enlisted men's club until dinnertime, then piled into Dent's and Graber's cars for the freeway ride to Pacific Grove, where they wiled away the evenings drinking beer and watching their rented television. Weekends, they ranged up and down the coast from San Francisco to Big Sur, on the lookout for girls and for wineries dispensing free samples. Except for their Army pay, they felt and acted like ordinary office workers. Best of all, every golden day meant one less in Southeast Asia.

Pringle was buoyantly pleased with himself: his stock with Finance, Medical Records, and Overseas Replacement had reached new heights; the translators, settled snugly into jobs on the post, were safe; and Captain Archer, despite his misgivings, had come around. Everything seemed to be turning out nicely.

Then, at the end of May, four months after the appearance of the translators, another batch of five arrived from Fort Bliss—they, too, had been disqualified as interrogators.

"Dammit, Lew!" Captain Archer said. "They can't *all* be spooks. What the hell's going on here?"

"Jesus, Archie, I don't know."

"And stop calling me Archie."

"Yes, Sir," Pringle said meekly.

"Get rid of them."

"We can't move them without authorization from Washington."

"I don't give a shit. Get 'em outta here or you might find *your* ass shipping out."

The trouble was that the translators' section chiefs didn't want to let them go. "Jesus Christ," Staff Sergeant Dreyfuss complained, "I've built my whole operation around these guys. Take 'em away and I'm up shit creek."

"Don't worry," Pringle said soothingly. "I've got five more and I'll let you have two."

Pringle stalled for a week before mustering the nerve to broach the subject with his contact at the Pentagon by gingerly alluding to the new arrivals from Fort Bliss.

"Train 'em and ship 'em, same as the others. When did they go over?"

Pringle paused. "The translators?" he said sheepishly. "Great guys, really terrific. We've got two in Finance, two in Medical Records, and two in Overseas Replacement."

"Dipshit. You've still got them?"

"Uh . . . ," Pringle sighed after an uncomfortable silence.

"Do you know how much it cost to teach those sonofabitches to speak Vietnamese? You've been sitting on half a million dollars worth of military equipment that should have been in Viet Nam months ago. Ship their ass out!"

"Okay, okay," Pringle said defensively.

"RIGHT NOW!"

"I found a way to get rid of them," Pringle reported to Captain Archer that afternoon. "Just say the word and they're out of here."

"Cut the orders and send them on their way. I suppose they'll have to be paid first?"

They would. And it would take at least three days to straighten out their records so they could clear post. Now, all Pringle had to do was tell the translators that their luck had run out. He phoned the Overseas Replacement Station and asked Grote to stop by his office.

"They caught up with us," he told Grote. "We gotta let you go."

"It had to happen eventually. You bought us some time and we appreciate what you did for us."

"Your orders are for next Monday, but you can leave Friday morning. That'll give you three extra days."

They shook hands. In the past, Pringle had routed thousands of soldiers to Viet Nam without ever having a second thought. Now, for reasons he didn't entirely understand, he'd saved the translators four months in the jungle and it gave him an unexpected sense of well-being.

"Good luck over there, Tim," he said.
"Thanks. I'll tell the others."

When Grote had gone, Pringle spread the new translators' files out on his desk and began poring over them.
These guys, he told himself, he'd hide so deep that nobody could ever find them.

Welcome to the Hothouse

TIMOTHY Grote didn't know a soul on the plane.

The flight from Travis Air Force Base, California, to Viet Nam took twenty hours, and having crossed the international dateline, they arrived on the afternoon of the day after they left. A late June snow was falling when they stopped to refuel in Anchorage, and Grote was tempted to send a postcard home, but it seemed like too much trouble. The plane also refueled in Japan—as it descended for its approach, Grote peered out the window at the bustling traffic below and thought about Bataan, Guadalcanal, and Nagasaki. He bought a dry, tasteless hamburger and a milk shake in the snack bar, then sat on a bench and smoked cigarettes until it was time to reboard the plane.

Next stop: Saigon.

Theirs was a commercial flight, and Grote stared longingly at the stewardesses in their bright yellow minidresses. He watched one in particular, a long-legged, tight-breasted blonde, thinking how much he'd like to bend her over one of the seats and flip the skimpy skirt up over her plump buttocks. Catching him looking, she smiled, and he grinned back foolishly. She knew what it was all about. Look at this, boys. Remember these round eyes, these dazzling legs, my elegant ass. Just one year, a measly 365 days, and then you can go back to the world and screw yourselves blind. That is, unless you get yourselves killed or your dicks blown off.

The airliner circled around and behind a huge, high thunderhead, then slipped underneath it to approach

Saigon from the west, and Grote got his first glimpse of Viet Nam. Despite the snakes and tigers and centipedes and little men with Russian rifles and other obnoxious things he couldn't see but knew were down there, the lush green forest *was* beautiful. Then, through the rain-spattered window, he began to notice tiny, vulnerable base camps and firebases, and thought, Sweet Jesus, not there—don't make me go to one of those forlorn places where people get slaughtered. When the plane had taxied to a stop, the blonde he'd been watching stood at the front of the cabin with a microphone in her hand.

"On behalf of the captain, crew, and myself, I'd like to welcome you to Ton Son Nhut International Airport." She paused until the chorus of booing and derisive laughter died down. "The captain has informed me that the ground temperature is ninety-seven degrees and it's raining. The correct time is ten minutes past four. For those of you in the rear of the plane, that means the big hand is on two and the little hand is on four. We've enjoyed serving you today and hope your stay in the Republic of Viet Nam is a pleasant one and that you'll join us soon for a return flight."

Amidst another chorus of booing, Grote, along with a few of the others, stared incredulously at the girl.

As he crossed the tarmac with the others, his new jungle fatigues felt clammy in the steamy heat and gently falling rain. Near the seedy terminal building, they came upon an equal number of men, sullen and weary: these would occupy their seats when the plane returned to California. The men were seated on long benches, some sleeping with their heads tipped forward, others staring blankly at the new arrivals. Their fatigues were faded and torn, their boots battered beyond repair. They looked used up, incredibly old, vanquished.

"Sorry we're late," somebody from Grote's group sang out. "We stopped in Yakoda for pizza and beer." This was followed by scattered, nervous laughter. A black Spec Five in a tattered bush hat slowly rose and glared at the speaker, livid eyes glinting dully from within hollow, gray sockets. Except for the effort required, he looked as if he'd be as happy as not to kill the wise guy with his bare hands.

"Motherfucker don't know *shit*," he hissed. "*You'll* see, you mother." Then he resumed his seat, staring vacantly toward the runway, his gaze extending out beyond it to where a low line of trees stretched along the horizon.

The Army bus they boarded was air-conditioned and the windows were covered by steel-mesh screens to ward off hand grenades and casually tossed bombs. Even with the windows closed, Grote could smell it— the faint, foul tropical odor, fertile and ominous, like the bottomland down by the river when he was a kid. During the trip to Long Binh and the 90th Replacement Battalion, Grote was unprepared for the squalor and poverty of the place, which brought to mind the shantytowns outside Port of Spain. Tumbledown shacks, slapped together from scraps of wood, corrugated steel, plywood, flattened tin cans, even cardboard, were scattered haphazardly along the roadside. The Vietnamese, in black pajama trousers, shapeless gray blouses, and conical straw hats, seemed indistinguishable. Some carried umbrellas as they made their way gingerly through the abiding and oily mud; others merely squatted on their haunches in front of their hovels, glancing up contemptuously as the busload of American soldiers continued its progress.

"Jesus," somebody said from the rear, "*look* at this fucken dump."

Feeling more alone than ever before in his life, Timothy Grote was.

He'd been sitting on his duffel bag for nearly three hours, in the shade of a metal-roofed pavilion outside the air-conditioned Personnel Office at the replacement battalion, waiting for his ride out to the 5th Bat-

talion, 2nd Field Forces Artillery, the Duster compound. "What's a Duster?" he'd asked the sergeant
who handed him his orders.

"Two 40-millimeter cannons mounted on a track,
like pom-pom guns in old war movies."

"What do they do?"

"Kick gook ass."

"What do they want with me?"

"How the fuck should I know? You'll find out soon
enough."

He studied the map on the wall outside the Personnel Office; next to it was a chart showing where the
units were headquartered and explaining what they
did. The 5th Battalion comprised four Duster batteries,
a searchlight battery, and a battery of quad-fifties—
Grote didn't know what they were, either. The Duster
batteries had their headquarters at places like Cu Chi,
Xuan Loc, and Ho Nai, and formed a straight line
across the country, forty miles north of Saigon. Under
Mission the chart read: CONVOY ESCORT DUTY, SEARCH
AND DESTROY, TACTICAL SUPPORT.

It had rained earlier, but the sun was out now and
the mud had changed back to fine dust. Grote was
sweaty and miserable, and the cigarettes he smoked
burned his mouth and tongue. He was thirsty and
wished for a can of beer but couldn't even walk the
hundred yards to the EM club because he'd be AWOL
if his ride showed up and he wasn't where he was supposed to be. His new steel helmet with its camouflage
cover lay on the ground next to him—he tried to pick
it up but jerked his hand away when he touched it. He
kicked it back into the shade and dragged his duffel bag
out of the sun, which had moved and caught him out
in the open.

At 3:30, a mud-caked three-quarter-ton truck crept
slowly toward the pavilion, growling in low gear. Two
men wearing floppy bush hats bounced in the cab, the
one on the passenger's side holding an M-16. The truck
stopped, and the one with the rifle took his hat off and

leaned out of the cab, tanned and blond, looking like a recruiting poster.

"You the newby?"

"I don't think so. My name's Grote."

The man took a piece of paper from his pocket, unfolded it, and then glanced back at Grote. "Throw your shit in the back and get in."

Before leaving Long Binh, they stopped at the PX, and the blond one handed Grote his rifle, then went inside. Grote sat on the wooden-slatted seat behind the cab, feeling the heft of the rifle in his hand, half in awe of the power of destruction it represented. The driver turned around and poked his head through the rear window of the cab.

"I'm Mouse," he said, then turned back to the front.

The blond one returned with three cases of Budweiser, which he placed in the truck bed, then tossed something to Grote, a bush hat.

"Compliments of the Sergeant Major," he said. "We only wear our pots in the bunker."

"Thanks," Grote said hesitantly, trying the hat on and adjusting the strap under his chin.

"Not like that," the blond one said. "The strap goes behind your head."

Grote made the correction, looking to the blond soldier for approval. He nodded at Grote and extended his hand through the window. "I'm Ned," he said.

"Where are we going?"

"Home. For a few days, anyway, until they decide what to do with you. What's your M.O.S.?"

"Personnel," Grote said as Mouse started the truck, precluding further conversation as they rattled out of the PX lot, Grote, his gear, and their beer bouncing in the bed every time they hit a bump.

What Grote could have said, given the opportunity, was that two years earlier he'd been a graduate student at Michigan State, trying to teach English composition to reluctant students who themselves would try to teach the same subject in elementary schools scattered across the Midwest. When it looked as if he'd be drafted, he'd volunteered for the Peace Corps, only to be unceremoniously kicked out ("de-selected," the Peace Corps director had said) after a highly publicized drunken ramble through Port of Spain, Trinidad, with the minister of education from St. Kitts.

Then he was drafted and eventually sent to Texas for nine months to learn Vietnamese so that he could be further trained as an interrogator. But it turned out that Military Intelligence didn't want anything to do with former Peace Corps volunteers, even if they were, like Grote, misfits who couldn't be trusted not to disgrace themselves in nightclubs with ministers of education from tiny Caribbean nations. So the Army sent him to Fort Ord, California, for a personnel course, and promptly forgot about him. By the time the error was discovered it was almost too late: he was nine months from completing his two-year obligation. Still, they'd get eight months, the Army's pound of flesh, out of him in Viet Nam.

Jouncing in the back of the truck, Timothy Grote gazed balefully back toward Long Binh, wondering where in hell they were taking him. For the life of him, he couldn't remember what had seemed so amusing about climbing up on the stage with Dr. Baldridge, the both of them laughing uproariously and waving their shirts over their heads as they tried to kiss the strippers, Grote calypso-dancing his way out of the Peace Corps and twelve thousand miles around the world to this godforsaken hothouse.

There was an unreality about what was happening and what had happened thus far, like his first night in the replacement battalion, when he lay on an upper bunk with his boots on, sopping with sweat, hearing the pop of flares and watching their glare move on the wall as they descended, dangling from tiny parachutes. There had been no shooting, just the flares and the rumble of trucks and gabble of people talking in the night. Still,

and this is what baffled Grote, he'd felt strangely content to be back in the tropics again.

Mouse turned off the pavement and they passed
through a checkpoint manned by Americans, then pro-
ceeded along a dusty road, seeing more Vietnamese and
fewer Americans. They passed through another checkpoint and after that there were no more Americans.
Grote put his face close to the window of the cab.

"How much farther?" he yelled as they bumped
slowly over the tracks where the road angled sharply
beside a ramshackle rail station.

"Another couple miles," Ned yelled back. "We've
been circling Long Binh's perimeter. One of the things
we do is cover their ass end with artillery. They got
their butts kicked during Tet."

Ahead, Grote could see a broad, shallow, defoliated
valley and, in the pale, distant, coppery haze, what
appeared to be a jumble of dilapidated outbuildings
perched atop a small rise. He tapped Ned's shoulder.

"That's not it, is it?"

"Sho 'nuf, Sunshine," Ned said. "If you get lucky,
that's home for the next twelve months."

Eight, Grote thought as he resumed his seat, facing
the rear. Eight months. He shook his head and closed
his eyes.

There were others in the transit hootch with him that
night, younger than he and straight out of Artillery
School. They drank beer and joked nervously while
heating cans of pork and beans over Sterno burners.
They would be combat troops and he would not, and
when they discovered this they closed ranks, politely
excluding him. Fair enough, Grote thought; his odds
were a hell of a lot better than theirs. He removed his
boots and lay on the bare mattress, staring up at the
corrugated roof of the hootch, feeling singular and
alone. Eventually, the others settled in for the night,
and the darkened hootch echoed with the sounds of
fitful snoring.

At 2:30, Grote crashed awake to booming artillery and panic in the transit hootch.

"What the fuck's going on?" somebody bawled in the darkness.

"Mom!" a young voice whined plaintively.

The heavy pounding sounded like BOOM . . . ssss, BOOM . . . ssss. Ours, Grote thought—if they were incoming, they'd go ssss . . . BOOM. From the sound of it, they were firing across the compound from the far end, right over their heads. He was about to tell the others when a roving guard entered the hootch, letting the screen door slap shut behind him. "Quiet down, Newbies!" the guard hollered. "Those are our 105s at the other end of the compound. Go back to sleep. Pretend it's thunder."

"What if I'm afraid of thunder?" one of the artillerymen said.

"Then you're shit out of luck."

Before drifting back to sleep, Grote concentrated on the sounds of small-arms fire crackling in the distance, punctuated by occasional machine-gun bursts. In the brief, eerie glow provided by flares, he could see the faces of the artillerymen, beardless and innocent, more like boys in Army suits than killers, and he sighed at the waste. He didn't know what the shooting was all about, but reckoned they wouldn't be left defenseless in the transit hootch if there was any real danger.

"RATS!" somebody screamed at four o'clock. "The fucken place has rats!"

A flashlight beam swept across the floor, and Grote was able to focus his eyes in time to catch a glimpse of the repulsive pink tail and furry haunches as they disappeared through a hole in the floor.

"What did you expect, asshole? I told you not to bring food in here."

"I was hungry."

"So was the rat."

Grote folded his arms across his chest and shut his

eyes tightly, trying to will himself to sleep before daybreak. Conceding the futility of it, he swung his legs
over the edge of the cot and fumbled for a cigarette,
knowing he'd smoke one after another until breakfast.

It was nearly time for lunch when Grote, bleary-eyed
and unshaven, was interviewed by Ned. Despite the
fierce heat, he could have slept anywhere. Ned's fa-
tigue shirt and dog tags hung on a nail behind his desk,
and his O.D. T-shirt was soaked.

"What'd you do at Fort Ord?"

"Processed overseas replacements. My last job was
processing myself."

"I think we're gonna keep you. Binkers wants to talk
to you. If he says okay, you can room with me."

"And if he doesn't?"

"He will."

Mr. Binks, the warrant officer who ran the Personnel
Section, had a round, bland face and a sandy mustache,
and spoke with a New England accent. He studied
Grote's 201 File, then laid it on the desk and chuckled.

"So close, so close," he said. "You almost made it,
Grotey—two more months and they wouldn't have
shipped you. Bad luck, Grotey, rotten bad luck. If you
work out, we've got an E-5 slot that needs filling before
they take it away from us. Ned'll show you around."

Relieved that, for the time being anyway, things
weren't going to get any worse, Grote thanked Mr.
Binks and asked what his duties would be. Mr. Binks
dismissed him with a wave of his hand. "We'll work
you in somehow. The first thing to do is get yourself
acclimated."

On his way to the mess hall, Grote was almost
cheerful. He'd been in Viet Nam five days so far, nothing bad had happened, and he'd landed a job on a compound with a lot of firepower. And for the next eight
months he'd be Grotey.

After lunch he reported to the Quartermaster, where
he was issued a rifle and ammunition, an armored vest,

a poncho, mosquito net, bedding, and a small plastic bottle of insect repellent. Back in the hootch, he made up his cot and put his other things away, then peeled off his sweaty jungle fatigues and put on a pair of cut-offs. Then, rubber thongs slapping against his heels, he sauntered the two hundred yards to the latrine with a towel draped over his neck, to shave and take his first shower in six days.

The ceiling of the jury-rigged shower room was inhabited by thousands of spiders, some as large as small crabs. Grote watched them warily, until he satisfied himself that they'd stay up there where they belonged and noted that they seemed more interested in eating each other than in dropping down to bite him. Even so, if he had to choose between spiders and snakes, he'd take spiders any day.

The water that trickled from the pipe overhead was cold, but Grote didn't mind—it felt too good to be clean again. He remembered his mother sobbing and pounding her fist on the kitchen table when he had to leave to catch his plane for San Francisco. If this was war, it didn't feel like it yet. He twirled under the weak stream to rinse the soap off his body, shuffling his feet and shaking his shoulders to a half-remembered calypso tune. He'd write home when he got back to the hootch. He turned the water off, but found that he was sweating too much to dry himself. Then, feeling as irrelevant as a bad pun, Timothy Grote toweled himself off as best he could before heading back across the Duster compound to his new home and who-knew-what lay in store for him.

Next morning, he was brushing his teeth next to the spigot that extended upward from a pipe that paralleled the ditch behind the hootch. At the edge of his peripheral vision, he perceived movement, and when he turned he saw a two-foot-high flame dancing to and fro in a metal box. Toothbrush in hand, he approached the three men who stared with evident satisfaction at the flame, which paused at one end of the box, lurched spasmodically, then remained stationary. The box turned out to be an animal trap, the kind gardeners use when they want to catch rabbits and other pests but don't want to hurt them, with doors at the ends that drop shut when the animal takes the bait. The rat had apparently been caught during the night, then doused with kerosene and set on fire in the morning. Grote studied the smoldering rodent for a moment, then glanced at the three men, two of whom he recognized from the Personnel Section, and returned to the ditch to finish brushing his teeth.

After lunch, Ned told him to hurry and get his rifle.

"What's up?" Grote hadn't heard any sirens.

"Initiation time, Grotey. We're going for a walk."

Rifles slung over their shoulders, Grote, Ned, and two other men from the Personnel Section approached the main gate, where they were waved on by smirking guards. Outside the wire and past the minefield, they marched single file for a hundred yards, then turned off the dirt road and onto a narrow path that ran through waist-high sawgrass until they reached a meager grove of stunted bamboo. There, a Vietnamese prostitute of indeterminate age squatted on a camouflage poncho liner, holding aloft a yellow parasol with two broken ribs. At the approach of the four Americans, she grunted something that Grote translated as "pigs," then grinned lewdly, revealing teeth stained black from chewing betel nut. When Ned pointed at Grote, she lifted her *ao dai* over her waist, then leaned back, as if in anticipation.

The Colonial

I always had a knack for languages. In high school, I studied Latin and French; in college, German and Spanish. When I was drafted, I was a graduate student in comparative literature. I was sent to California to study Vietnamese for eight months, and then I was trained as an interrogator in Maryland. My first job in Viet Nam was to oversee twelve old women who filled sandbags.

They really didn't have to be guarded, but there was supposed to be an American in charge. They wore rubber thongs, black pajama trousers, shapeless gray shirts, and conical straw hats. Their teeth were black and shiny from the betel nuts they chewed constantly. I spent most of my time sitting in what shade I could find, reading and smoking. Occasionally, I would have to excuse one of them so she could go to the Vietnamese latrine at the edge of the compound.

In the beginning, I tried to carry on conversations with them but soon gave up. All they wanted to talk about were the young girls they could get for me. Three dollars, one of them told me. One for me, two for the girl. You want? Some other time, I said.

They lined up outside our gate at 6:30 and worked until 11:00. Then they ate lunch and worked some more until 3:00. We paid them a dollar in cash every day, and when they went away, their scrunched up, monkeylike faces showed no signs of gratitude.

Can't somebody else do it? I said when my name appeared again on the duty roster. I'm an interrogator.

That's your problem, not mine, the First Sergeant

said, looking up from his desk. We don't have any prisoners. Quit bitching. His huge, fat neck glistened with sweat and there was a wet spot where his hand rested on some papers in front of him. It was rumored that he drank a fifth of bourbon every night.

I can do other things. There must be something else you can find for me to do.

I don't give a rat's ass what you can do, he said. You'll find plenty to do before it's time to go. Take it easy while you've got the chance.

For five weeks, I watched the women. Occasionally, there would be something to break the monotony. Sometimes I went to the village with the civil affairs team; other times I worked in the aid station with the medics, although that didn't turn out very well. If we'd had a prisoner, I could have asked him how many men were in his unit, how many machine guns, officers, antitank weapons, where he came from, that sort of thing. Nothing in my language training had prepared me to ask a woman what was wrong with her sick child.

I began to stay late at the air-conditioned NCO club. If I drank enough gin I could get to sleep fairly soon after returning to my room. The waitresses, who were checked twice a week by the medics, would go into a back room for six dollars. I was usually content to sit at the bar and get quietly drunk and then go home to let my fan blow over me for the rest of the night.

I went about my work guarding the women, reading, and bumming around the medics' hootch. I nailed shell crates to the wall in my room to make bookcases and began to build a collection of paperback books, stolen from the USO library. I bought a woven mat in the village to use as a carpet. Soon, I had a chest of drawers and a bamboo curtain. I found an old broken table and used it for a desk. Despite my degrading work, I began to feel that civilization was possible, even in Viet Nam when there was a war going on.

There were reminders from time to time that we

were in a war zone. You could hear screaming and
small-arms fire coming from the village sometimes,
and one night an ARVN corporal killed his wife because she slept with Americans when he was out in
the field. Another time a helicopter went roaring by
and began firing just off our south perimeter, lighting
up the whole area with its searchlight and making a
tremendous noise. We weren't completely cut off from
the war; we just weren't involved in it very much.

One day the bamboo curtain clicked furiously as the
First Sergeant pushed his way in. He looked at what I'd
done in my room, shook his head, and turned to leave.
I want to see you in my office, he said. Then, as an
afterthought, You better not be smoking any of that
bad shit in here.

On Mondays and Thursdays a truck came to collect
trash from the compound. Our commander suspected
Vietnamese trashmen of being the conduit for the ra-
dios, watches, clothing, toilet articles, and other goods
that were being stolen from the compound. Whenever
we checked our civilian employees they were clean,
but the thefts continued unabated. It had to be the garbagemen, our commander reasoned.

Take your rifle and stroll along casually, the First
Sergeant said. Keep your eyes and ears open and don't
let on that you speak gook. See what you can find out.

The sandbaggers, I said. They'll tell on me.

We'll fire them. Give somebody else a chance to
make a few bucks. Kind of spread the wealth around,
he said and began to laugh derisively.

Later that afternoon I heard wailing and crying when
they were fired. The S-5 officer said they could come
back in a few weeks to cut grass and that quieted them.
As they were leaving they looked at me sullenly, and
one of them asked me if I wanted her to get me a boy.
Ba gnu nhu bo, I said. Stupid cow.

I followed the garbage truck at a distance of five yards,
my rifle slung over my shoulder. The garbage, which
had accumulated for four days, stank in the tropical

heat. As the Vietnamese unloaded refuse from the fifty-gallon oil drums, giant cockroaches and other crawly things scurried for cover. There was a dead snake in one of the barrels, and the boy who took the cover off shrieked and ran away from it. He jabbered in Vietnamese, saying the bastard Americans had done it on purpose. I looked at the ground, trying not to laugh, and an older man told the boy to shut up.

Well, said the First Sergeant, what did you find out?

They're afraid of snakes, but they don't seem to mind centipedes. They didn't steal anything today.

Keep an eye on them. Maybe they were nervous.

None of the civilian employees approached the truck when I was following it. The fifth time out, one of the garbagemen took a clean cardboard box from a trash barrel and placed it carefully in the garbage truck. *Ong kia noi tieng Viet Nam khong?* the driver said. Is he the one? *Phan!* another said. Shit. I looked at the ground, pretending to be interested in a piece of fruit that was covered with tiny ants.

There's not much to it, I said. They drop the stuff off in cardboard boxes and the garbagemen take it out. They were testing me today; that box was probably empty.

Next time we'll catch them red-handed, the First Sergeant said. Work the fuckers over.

Thursday it rained and I slogged through the mud with my rifle tipped down to keep water out of the barrel. I knew where the drop points were, and we had men waiting at each one. They would emerge at my signal and we would take the garbagemen into custody. A small box was picked up at the first drop, and two larger ones at the second. At the third, the driver got out and helped them lift something heavy into the truck.

I chambered a shell and pointed my rifle at them. *Het roi*, I said. All finished. You guys are dead.

Du me, the driver said. Fuck.

Please, sir, don't shoot, the other one said when

we'd lined them up against the truck. The other two didn't say anything. In the boxes were two watches, a portable radio, several washcloths, and some bars of soap. The heavy box had a tape recorder and a pair of size-six jungle boots.

Ong biet noi tieng My khong? I said. You speak English?

Yes, sir.

Cac ong biet noi tieng My khong? And the others?

Da phai. He nodded.

What the hell's going on here? the First Sergeant said.

They all speak English.

Spies, eh?

They wouldn't admit it if they were. They're probably just thieves.

I'm not taking any chances. I sent for an interrogation team from Cu Chi. He went over to the one I'd been talking to and pushed him back against the truck. You little yellow fucker, he said. We'll find out what your game is.

We left the truck where it was and took them out behind the Orderly Room and tied their hands behind their backs and made them squat in the mud while we waited for the interrogators to arrive. When they did, they had some MPs with them and they took the Vietnamese away in the back of a three-quarter-ton truck. Some other Vietnamese came from the village to drive the garbage truck.

I could have done it, I said. You didn't have to call in those guys from Cu Chi.

I wanted pros, the First Sergeant said.

That's my job. I was trained to do that.

Shit, he said.

Three days later we learned that the garbagemen had been freed.

The man on the Vespa returns to haunt me. I am riding in a truck to Long Binh with Jenkins. I have heard that there are eleven small refrigerators at the 2nd Field Forces PX and I am going to buy one for my room. Jenkins, with two years of college, is going to get the mail. To my right, a Vietnamese appears, riding a small motorcycle alongside the truck. He looks familiar, although I might be imagining it. He smiles, nods, almost seems to bow in our direction. His right arm hangs at his side because of the small package he carries.

Shoot the sonofabitch! Jenkins says.

What?

Shoot the motherfucker. He's got a bomb. Jenkins starts swerving the truck back and forth across the road, trying to bump the Vietnamese so we can get away. Incredibly, he stays with us, although he's riding the motorcycle with only one hand. I know now why he looks familiar—he is one of the garbagemen we caught stealing. I pull the slide back on the .45 and try to push it, but it won't go. I pull it back again and release it and it slams forward.

God damn it. God damn it! Jenkins is shouting at me. Shoot! I can't keep doing this all day.

I stick the .45 out the window, but with the truck going all over the place I can't aim. Go straight so I can aim, I tell him.

I point the pistol at the Vietnamese's face and he still smiles. He swings closer and starts to raise his arm. From a distance of six feet, I fire, hitting him in the chin, and that part of his jaw disappears. He tries to throw the package and I fire again, hitting him in the stomach and doubling him up. The wheel of the Vespa pivots, and man and machine fall in a heap in the middle of the road. I turn to look through the rear window of the truck and there are two muffled explosions. One is a small bomb and the other is the gas tank of the Vespa.

Thank god, Jenkins says. You're lucky he had a bomb. You could have gotten in a lot of trouble if he didn't.

It ends with a crowd of Vietnamese women surrounding the truck, waving their arms over their heads and shouting. They close in on us, the mothers of sick children from the medics' hootch, the sandbaggers, the waitresses from the NCO club, the grass cutters. They have the mangled body of the garbageman raised high in the air. *Anh cua chung toi*, they sigh. *Ong giet Anh cua chung toi.* You killed our man. I climb to the hood of the truck and wave my pistol. Go on! Get out of our way! I shout. I aim the .45 over their heads and try to fire, but it is out of shells and the hammer clicks impotently.

After a routine investigation I was awarded a Bronze Star—for conspicuous bravery, it read on the citation— and Jenkins got an Army Commendation Medal—his second, the first having been awarded for mailroom efficiency. He was angry because he didn't get a Bronze Star too. Our commanding officer pinned the medals on us at noon formation one day, but we had to give them back after the ceremony. Your awards will be issued to you when you get back to the States, the First Sergeant said.

Two weeks later I was reassigned to an artillery battery in Xuan Loc as a clerk.

You're an interrogator, the First Sergeant said. There's nothing for you to do. Besides, everyone in the village knows you killed that guy. You're a liability around here.

I don't want to go to Xuan Loc. I've got my room fixed up and everything.

I don't give a shit what you want. I don't want to get my ass blown off because you wasted some gook garbage collector. There's not much going on there— you'll be okay.

I sold most of my stuff but kept my refrigerator and fan. In the morning I had to load the truck alone, and then had to wait until after lunch for a driver to be free. At the gate I lit a cigarette and looked the place over for the last time. Near the south perimeter the same twelve old women were filling sandbags, under the direction of an overseer who took his job seriously. Rifle

slung over his shoulder, he walked among them, stopping from time to time to examine their work. One of
them looked in my direction and I took off my hat and
waved. She spat a stream of betel juice and turned back
to the mound of sand.

Statement

WELL, I was sittin in a empty bunker, y'know. Takin a little sham time. It was Sunday, after all. I was entitled. Shit, they work us every day here, anyway. Ya gotta take your breaks when you can. I'm sittin there havin a smoke and I hear em start comin in. KA WHAM! KA WHAM! KA WHAM!

So I hit the dirt. What else ya gonna do? Ya gotta look out for number one, right? I was layin there wishin I was underground, like in a ditch or something. You're safer underground. A good mortarman can drop one in a rain barrel from four hundred meters. And they got em. Them gook mortarmen is as good as any we got. Below ground level there's no way in hell you're gonna get hurt. Unless he drops in on your head. And he won't do that. He'd rather hit a building. Charlie knows what hurts.

There wasn't no place to go so I stayed in the bunker waiting for it to be over. They can't keep it up for long. Especially during the day. I knew it wouldn't be long and I'd hear the choppers so I just laid there and waited. I don't know why they decided to hit us. We didn't do nothin to bother them. And on a Sunday. A goddamn Sunday. Shit, they don't respect nothin. The choppers would come and tear up some gook ass. I knew that.

Pretty soon I heard the flapping of the chopper blades and I knew it would be done soon. I didn't hear any small-arms fire so I knew there wasn't going to be no ground attack. They just wanted to drop a few in on us to let us know they were around. Then I hear the choppers open up with their fifties. Braaaaghk!

Braaaaghk! Them fuckin miniguns can't be stopped. If Charlie knew we had those things he never woulda started this war. I'm still laying there, but I feel comfortable because I know it will be over soon. They usually call the choppers out from Long Binh someplace. Anyway, they finally got there and started ripping Charlie up.

By now I know I don't have anything to worry about so I decide to have a smoke and tell them I was in the latrine when it happened. That's good enough, I was thinking. I wasn't gone long when it happened. So I light up a smoke and lean back against the wall of the bunker, lookin out the door. Across the way I could see the chapel and the basketball court. I was just relaxin. Pretty soon the all-clear siren begins wailin and I know I can go back to the Personnel Section, where I work. Drivin the truck.

I stepped out of the bunker and wished I didn't. There, walkin towards me, comes Barman. Lieutenant Barman, I mean. He spots me right off and I see there's going to be trouble. He walked real fast.

"Minary," he says. "What are you doing here?" His voice was real stern, like he thought I did something wrong.

"I was in the latrine," I said. "When I heard em comin in I ran out here."

"The latrine is two hundred yards away," he said in that New York accent of his. There's nothin, I mean nothin, more aggravating than the way a New York Jew talks. So superior and all.

He wants me to say something, but I didn't say a word. I just waited for him to unload on me. He looked at me real hard and I started to feel like maybe I did do something wrong. It didn't last, though. I know that's the way they want you to feel. I just stared at him, waiting.

"They dropped one in on the Personnel hootch. Get your ass back there and see if you can help them clean up," he said.

"Yes, Sir," I said, and started off.

"Minary!" he yelled and I stopped and looked back at him. "When you mop up the blood, remember where you were when they were dying."

Shit, I thought. That fuckin Jew bastard wants me to feel guilty. Fuck him. It's every man for himself. You got to look out for number one, right? How was I supposed to know Charlie'd hit us today? It wasn't my fault. He didn't have any right to try and make me feel like that. I felt pretty low by the time I got back to the hootch. And it was Barman's fault. I didn't do anything wrong.

I didn't see him for some time after that. I was just doin my job and keepin out of trouble. The best way to get by is just do your job and don't bother nobody. Then one night I have guard duty in the observation tower. I liked that fine. The tower is way up in the air and you don't get bugs up there. A few bats, maybe, but they don't bother you much. Only, when it rains, the tower is the worst place to be. The water comes in every-place. It was the dry season, though, so I was happy to be in the tower.

Barman's the Officer of the Guard. I didn't mind that much. I figured I wouldn't see him all night. There ain't many officers'll climb that ladder to the tower. I admit, I didn't like the son of a bitch. We stood guard formation and Barman comes along and looks at my rifle.

"Minary," he says. "Your rifle's dirty."

"Yes, Sir," I said.

"You're going to need this rifle someday and it won't be any good to you. Clean it."

"Yes, Sir," I said.

"I want you to clean this weapon before you go to your post. And show it to me before you report."

"Yes, Sir," I said. And I'm thinkin, you bastard. What's it to you if I don't clean my rifle? It's no skin off your big nose. He was just a punk lieutenant and he was acting like he knew it all.

I went to the hootch and cleaned my rifle. Then I

had to run all over hell to find him and show it to him. It was an order, after all. And I didn't want no Article Fifteen or nothin like that. It was clean, too.

"Okay," he says. "You can report to your post." And I thought, is that all? That's it? He was just hasslin me. He didn't care about my rifle. He just wanted to bust balls on me.

I had the third watch. From eleven to one. The two other guys was sleepin and I was sittin in the chair lookin out over the area. There's a fight over towards Firebase Bearcat, and I watched the flares for a while thinkin about what it would be like to be in a fire fight at night. It must be scary as shit. It was far away, though, and I was just watchin the show. There was a cool sort of breeze and it was comfortable up there.

Then I hear it. Chink chunk. Chink chunk. There's somebody climbin up the ladder. Sixty feet in the air. Oh, fuck, I thought. So I went over to the side of the tower and looked down. It was Barman. That fool was climbin up the ladder. Probably no one told him he didn't have to do it. Climbin the ladder to the tower. I never saw any officer do that before.

He's alone. He musta been walkin the rounds of the bunkers because there wasn't any jeep around. I would've seen the jeep. Or heard it. I decided to have a little fun with the son of a bitch. I got my rifle and took the magazine out. It didn't have any shells in it. I leaned over the side of the tower.

"Halt!" I said. "Who's there?" Then I pulled the bolt back and let it slam to. You can't mistake that sound.

"It's the Officer of the Guard."

"I don't know that. What's the password?"

"Branch—stream," he says. "Minary. That you?"

"Yeah," I says. "It's me. Watchu doin up here?" He was close enough to see it.

"Put your rifle away. It's me," he said.

"Yeah, I know," I said. "You just turn your ass around and climb down the tower and don't come back."

"You could be court-martialed for that," he said in a officer voice. He was tryin to bluff me.

"You don't have no witnesses. I got a brick up here I could drop on your head and you'd fall and nobody'd be the wiser. Get down!"

He looked at me for a minute or two, like he was thinkin of something he could do to me. There wasn't nothin he could do, though. I had him and he knew it. It was just me and him and I had him beat. He looked at me with those black eyes of his and that big nose and I wanted to tell him I hated him and all officers and all Jews. Then he backed down. Just like them to back down.

"Minary," he said. "I'm going down. Don't shoot. I'm going down." And I thought, you chickenshit mother. A real man woulda faced me down. He wasn't worth shit, though.

After that I knew he was after me.

I didn't do anything wrong. Because I knew if he could pin anything on me he would. I stayed out of his way and did my job. He probably had the other officers watching me, too. I only had about five months left, with my extension, and I didn't want to have to stay there any longer than that. The Stockade counts as bad time; doesn't count towards getting out. They're smart and I knew he'd nail me if he could.

I was in the Personnel Office when I found out he was goin out to the field. I was so happy, just to know he was leaving. They were sending him to a line battery. Battery B, out in Cu Chi. That's a long way from us and I wouldn't see him again. He would be out of the way and he couldn't do nothin to me.

Then the Personnel Sergeant, Sergeant Giles, says to me I have to drive Barman out to Cu Chi. They didn't have no jeeps to spare and I could have the rest of the day off if I took him out to the battery. Shit, I didn't want to go out there. I told him I didn't know the way and he said not to worry, that Lieutenant Barman knew how to get there. There wasn't no way out. I had to go.

We started off the next morning. When Barman saw it was me who was drivin him he looked kind of pissed off, like he didn't want to go with me. Well, I didn't want to go either but there wasn't no way out. It was an order. So we get in the jeep and start off.

We drove through the countryside for a while, till we got to Long Binh. He tells me to drive on the base and stop at the Two Field Force PX because he needs some things to take with him. I thought, you dope, they got PXs at Cu Chi. They ain't got nothin here they ain't got there. It takes a while to get used to how things are in Viet Nam. I'll have to give him that. He just didn't know how things were.

When he came out of the PX he had a bag full of stuff that he put in the back of the jeep. And I thought, Oh, brother, this guy's got things to learn. The driving wasn't too bad. There wasn't much traffic, just a lot of those little Vespa buses filled with gooks and they get out of your way pretty fast or they get run down. As we got away from Long Binh the traffic thinned and we were rolling along pretty good. It was still early and it wasn't too hot yet. Barman had a pistol strapped on his waist and so did I. We both had rifles.

He reached back in the bag he brought and pulled out a bottle. It was whiskey. Goddamn Jack Daniels. He had some ice, too. He made a drink. Water from his canteen and whiskey and ice.

"Want a drink?" he said.

"Yes, Sir," I said. Hell, I'll have a drink anytime.

"Knock off that 'Sir' stuff. I know you, Minary. I know your kind. I've seen you before." I didn't know what he was talkin about. I mean, he was an officer and went to college and all.

He handed me a cup and I took a drink. "It's good," I told him. "Thank you, Sir."

"I said, cut the 'Sir' crap," he says. "Look, Minary. It's just me and you. We run into trouble and we're on our own. For a while, anyway, we need each other."

"I guess so," I said.

"You're goddamn right," he said. I'm thinkin, here I

am havin a drink with a officer and bullshittin and he's
a Jew. Hell, it's a long drive to Cu Chi. I might as well
try and get along with him. I couldn't understand him
givin me a drink. I wasn't nothin to him.

So we rode along like that for a while. Just drinkin
and riding. We were out in the country. There wasn't
too many vehicles on the road. It was pretty nice. I was
feelin pretty good.

"Where you from, Minary?" he said.

"Cincinnati," I said.

"They've got a good ball team there."

"You bet," I said. "That guy Bench is going to do
great things for them. Yeah. They're all right."

"I'm a Dodger fan," he said. "When I was a kid. Win
or lose, they were our heroes." He took his helmet off
and set it on the floor of the jeep. He was relaxin, I
could tell.

"Minary," he says after a while. "You don't like the
Army. Well, let me tell you somethin. I don't like it any
more than you do."

I nodded. "We're even on that score," I said.

"And I'm an officer and you don't like officers."

I nodded again.

"And I'm a Jew and you don't like Jews."

I was kind of surprised when he said that. I looked
at him and he looked right at me. I was goin to say
somethin but he cut me short.

"Well, none of that matters here. We're here and
there's nothin we can do about it. All we can do is try
to get along and stay alive until our time is up. The
only way we can make it is to work together."

I thought about that for a while and kept driving.

"Thanks for the drink," I said finally. "I really
mean it."

"That's all right," he said. "I make more money than
you do."

For a second I thought, yeah, just like a Jew. But I
don't think he meant it that way. So I didn't say anything. I just drove.

Then I heard this sound, like dropping a watermelon

on the sidewalk, and I looked over at Barman. He had this kind of scared look on his face and he was spilling his whiskey. I slowed the jeep down and reached over to grab the cup and he fell toward me. The other side of his head was gone. I never heard the shot or nothin. I pushed him back in his seat and stepped on the gas. We were about ten miles from Cu Chi and I hit sixty all the way.

The jeep was a mess by the time I got there. He shit his pants but I didn't even know it because we were drivin so fast. After I got there I knew what happened and felt bad about it. I spent a lot of time talkin to the Military Intelligence people but there wasn't nothin to be done. It was over. Whoever shot him was long gone. They'd never catch him.

I took the bottle of Jack Daniels from the back of the jeep and put it under the seat to bring back with me. Hell, there's no sense wastin good whiskey. Them MI people woulda just kept it for themselves. Ya gotta look out for number one, right? I mean, if you don't look out for number one, who's gonna do it?

The MPs found me a place to sleep that night and I drove back the next morning.

And that's all I have to say about it.

Warm Front

THAT night, Harvey Rutkus had guard duty. As they were milling around before guard mount, a Spec Four from the motor pool pointed to the sky. When they looked they could see, high in the air, sunlight glinting off the belly of a 707 as it made a wide, sweeping arc in its ascent before disappearing behind a ragged nimbostratus formation that portended rain.

"*Man*, did you see that freedom bird?" the Spec Four said. "I bet there's some happy dudes on that mother." Rutkus, the only Hebrew meteorologist in Quang Tin Province, still had more than half his tour to complete and didn't even want to think about it. He looked away and adjusted the extra bandolier of M-16 magazines slung over his shoulder, a concession to his father, who ended each of his weekly letters by admonishing his son that it was better to have too much ammunition than not enough.

Rutkus had been assigned to a middle bunker on the compound's west perimeter and was in a foul mood anyway. Behind them was Chu Lai, huge and sprawling; to the north lay an ARVN compound; and to the south, a wretched village whose name no one could pronounce. Nobody would attack from those directions, so if they got hit it would be from the west, where the low, flat plain stretched away toward the forest and a pimple-sized hill they called Mount Rushmore. The plain had been defoliated, but sawgrass and clumps of bushes had sprung up, providing plenty of cover. If anybody wanted to, they could sneak a whole company up to within two hundred yards of the perimeter. On the other perimeters you could relax and nobody minded; on the west you had to pay attention. The only good thing was that it was on high ground, so it was drier and had fewer mosquitoes.

He'd been over there a couple of times at night to drink beer and watch fire fights in the distance. Firebase Homer, five miles away, was pretty hot sometimes, and you could watch the gunships and Cobras working out, the tracers whisking through the air like roman candles. It had felt eerie to sit on the berm as a spectator, knowing his countrymen were fighting and there was nothing he could do about it. At the same time, Rutkus was glad he wasn't over there.

As a Spec Five, he was in charge, and he set the rotation as they trudged the four hundred yards to the bunker. He had two men with him: Reilly, a Spec Four from the Orderly Room, and a scrawny PFC from Scranton who nobody knew what to do with. At one time, he'd been assigned to an artillery battery as a clerk but was so incompetent and inept that they'd sent him back. He was a nice enough kid and spent his days hanging around the Personnel Section and Rutkus' weather shop, running errands when asked.

Scion of thirty generations of Lithuanian and American Jewry, Harvey Rutkus was twenty-five and, at six feet four and a hundred and seventy pounds, an improbable sight in jungle fatigues: a gangly weatherman with his head in the clouds. He walked with a shambling slouch, especially around the Vietnamese, and Lan, the girl who cleaned the hootch, said that from the side he looked like a map of Vietnam. Sometimes she'd go to bed with him, calling him Con Trau, which he thought was a nice nickname until he discovered it meant water buffalo. Still, he liked her well enough, and the vision of her slim, boyish hips and pert, virginal breasts would stay with him for days after he'd been with her, taking the edge off things.

His great-grandfather, a cabinetmaker, had emigrated from Lithuania prior to the turn of the century, opening a shop in Flatbush that initially prospered and then went into a slow decline. In 1922, Rutkus' grandfather transferred the business to Trenton, New Jersey, because he liked the name and was certain things would be better there. His grandfather's acumen and boldness loomed large in family chronicles, and he was credited with saving them all from ruin. Rutkus' father ran the furniture store now, the trade consisting largely of blue-collar workers and blacks. "Schwartzes," his father would say when anybody commented on this, "Schwartzes are good customers."

He'd been wounded at the Battle of the Bulge, three weeks before his son was born, and was holed up in Bastogne when the happy moment arrived. When Harvey was a boy and they'd go to the steam bath, he'd stare in awe and amazement at the ugly scar where the German bullet had slashed across his father's back, marveling at how much it must have hurt. "It doesn't hurt at the time," his father told him, "only later." Once, overhearing Harvey sneering at the goyim, he rebuked him sharply. "They saved my life," he said simply, and that was the end of it.

Unable to attend college himself, Rutkus' father was determined that his sons would. The younger of the two chose Rutgers, while Harvey, the sports zealot who would never amount to anything unless he cut loose from his mother's apron strings, settled on Michigan State because Earl Morrall had played there, and applied for a room in Snyder Dormitory as a sort of tribute to Duke Snider. His real hero, however, was Sandy Koufax, whose refusal to pitch on Yom Kippur left Harvey reeling with ethnic pride.

Rutkus' Jewishness was more sentimental than technical, something you were rather than something you did. He rarely attended services, in part because he was terrified of the MSU rabbi, an imposing figure in a gray crew cut who could have played linebacker. He observed the dietary laws when it was convenient but could indulge a weakness for bacon, lettuce, and tomato sandwiches without remorse. Two days before Passover, his junior year, he took the bus to a Jewish grocery in Lansing; then he and his roommate sat cross-legged on the floor of their ratty apartment drinking Mogen David, eating gefilte fish, and dipping boiled eggs from a bowl of salted water. But the hoked-up seder with a Midwest gentile fell flat, leaving Harvey with the theological equivalent of a bad taste in his mouth.

A history major, he approached the Second World War as one might an unexploded bomb. For his term project in modern European history, he researched the town his great-grandfather had left seven decades earlier, discovering that what his father told him was true. The Jews of Memel perished early, and the possibility that they had any relatives left in Europe was so remote as to be unimaginable. However, as monstrous as this seemed, it remained an abstraction: try as he might, he could not comprehend the physical reality of a mystery so heinous.

Unsure of himself after graduation, he worked alongside his father in the furniture store for the summer. By August he was bored and drove across Jersey's narrow neck to New Brunswick to try to wheedle his way into graduate school at Rutgers, only to discover on his return to Trenton that he'd been called up for his draft physical. It was then, in a nightmare moment of panic and haste, that he'd enlisted for four years, lured by the recruiter's pledge that he'd be sent to the Army's meteorological school in Arizona. Now, two and a half years later, he spent his days in an endless succession of data-gathering and reporting to the main shop on Chu Lai, from which he had been banished by Major Welch, a nasty anti-Semite.

He'd given himself the third watch, from eleven to one, and sat cross-legged on a low wooden platform, peering out through the horizontal gun slit and past the chain link fence that was supposed to make rocket grenades blow up before they got inside. Next to him on the platform, the bunker's light machine gun rested docilely on its bipod, breech coyly flipped open. The grenade launcher, its squat, stubby shells scattered like linemen after a play, looked like a toy. The drizzle he'd predicted fell softly, and he relaxed somewhat: no Vietnamese would want to go out on a night like this. Behind him, Reilly and the PFC from Scranton rested on wood-framed canvas cots, having exhausted themselves in aimless, trivial gossip.

If there was such a thing as a favorite time in Viet Nam, this was it. Alone with his thoughts, Rutkus could imagine himself anywhere in the world but where he was. Through the mist, the perimeter lights made him think of the Jersey Turnpike where it snaked past Newark. The minute he got back to Trenton, he'd commandeer his father's car and head straight to DiLorenzo's for a tomato pie. Or Levin's, where he'd order a whole plate of bagels and a quarter-pound of lox. Maybe he'd go to MacSorley's for dark ale, peanuts, and a cheese plate.

Five years earlier, just before their junior year, Tim Grote, Rutkus' collaborator in the misbegotten seder, had visited him and they'd driven to New York, ending up at MacSorley's, where they'd gotten drunk and almost didn't make it home to Trenton. Now Grote, the Michigan meshuggenah, was an interpreter down south somewhere in III Corps, having somehow managed to get himself drafted. It was Grote who'd told him that *Con Trau* meant "water buffalo," in a letter the previous week. He also reminded him of a bet they'd made in 1965: a case of beer that the war would be over by the time they graduated.

"Well, fuckstick," Grote had written, "here we are and you owe me a case of Budweiser."

If Rutkus ever saw Grote again, he'd pay the momzer off.

Having heard it so often, Rutkus could recite the litany of his father's adventure in the Ardennes forest from memory. At the upper end of the age scale for the draft, he probably could have avoided service altogether. However, at thirty-two and unaware that his wife's first pregnancy was just under way, he'd enlisted in the spring of 1944, expecting his experience in the furniture business to land him in the Quartermaster Corps. Instead, six days before Christmas, he stood knee-deep in snow, his carbine empty, staring incredulously into the spearhead of Model's advance. When the order was given to fall back, he slung his rifle over his shoulder and began to saunter leisurely in the direction of Bastogne, some ten kilometers to the west.

As GIs hotfooted it past him at a dead run, he began to jog awkwardly, trying to wring what he could from his weary body to keep up with the others. Halfway across an open meadow, machine-gun fire erupted from the edge of the forest, and Rutkus' father, reeling as if a giant hand had shoved him rudely from behind, sprawled clumsily in the snow and lay still, amazed and offended that somebody would actually shoot him.

He felt ridiculous lying there and bleeding all over the snow, hoping that when the Germans came by they'd think he was dead and leave him alone. He heard a tracked vehicle rumbling somewhere behind him and, assuming it was a German tank, willed himself motionless until he heard a distinctively midwestern accent bellow out a halt, then say, "He's still bleeding, so he ain't dead. Pick him up."

Three GIs whooshed through the snow, scooped him up, and then hoisted the over-age Jewish dogface onto the rear of a half-track. Somebody covered him with a stiff piece of canvas and said soothingly, "You're gonna be all right, buddy."

"Thanks, fellas," Rutkus' father murmured, and fainted.

And now, a quarter of a century later, his son shuddered in a tropical drizzle, smoking furtively behind his cupped hand so the glow from his cigarette wouldn't betray him, on the lookout for little yellow men brandishing Russian assault rifles.

At 11:30, a jeep carrying their wimpy executive officer sledded to a stop outside the bunker, and Rutkus' shpilkes went into remission. They usually called on the field phone before somebody came out, unless it was something important. Lieutenant Winkle was out of uniform, decked out in a garish Hawaiian shirt his wife had bought him during their R&R assignation on Maui.

"Who's in charge here?" Winkle said gruffly.

"I am, Sir."

"Pay attention," Winkle said, as if addressing a child. "We just got it from S-2 that you're gonna get socked tonight."

"In the *rain*? Aw, come on, Sir."

"Nothing big—they just want to let us know they're around and can do it. If they hit you here, return fire. The quad-fifty up the way will lay down a field of fire and you'll be okay."

"How about some help?"

"I'll send the roving guard over. They said it'd be between one and two. Like I said, it's no big deal."

"Just the roving guard? Jesus, Sir."

"You're in charge—take care of it." Winkle climbed back into the jeep and drove up the perimeter to where a crippled quad-fifty had been shoved into a ragged emplacement.

"Well, shit," Reilly said as the PFC from Scranton sat up and began rubbing his eyes. "What we gonna do, Boss?"

Because of the RPG fence, the grenade launcher would be useless inside the bunker, and nearly so out-side because it would take forever to calculate windage and elevation, so they'd have to rely on the machine gun. Rutkus would climb up on the roof with some flares to get a better view. If he saw anything, he'd pop a flare and the PFC from Scranton would cut loose with the machine gun, and Reilly, who was a better shot with a rifle, would open up with his M-16 on auto. While they were firing, Rutkus would pop another flare and get down from the roof. He set two boxes of M-60 ammunition next to the machine gun and opened them, pulling out one of the belts and laying it across the open breech.

"All you have to do is put the first shell in the

breech, close the top and push it down until it clicks, pull the bolt back, and you're ready to go," Rutkus said. "If I pop a flare and tell you to fire, you do it—I don't care if you see anything or not. I don't want to get stuck up there, so make lots of noise."

The roving guard arrived, simultaneously pissed off and grateful to have something to break the monotony of tramping around the compound when he'd rather be drinking beer in his hootch and playing poker. Rutkus explained the plan again, and when they said they'd got it he went outside.

"You guys with the rifles," he called back in, "I want one of you on either side of the machine gun."

The bunker was set into the berm, which sloped toward the rear, from about shoulder height at the front. Clutching his rifle and three flares, Rutkus crept up the berm on his hands and knees, then rolled onto the roof, which was sandbagged waist-high. Crouching awkwardly behind the sandbags, he realized that he'd have done better to send one of the shorter ones to the roof to take better advantage of the meager cover. Rutkus peered into the mist apprehensively, tense and alert, every molecule of his body *ready* for something. He watched and waited, watched and waited, more excited and alive than ever before in his life, as if everything that had ever happened to him was a preparation for this moment.

After five minutes, the feeling began to wane; after ten, it had faded almost completely; in twenty minutes he was bored, cramped, and soaked to the skin.

Then he saw something, slight movement a football-field's length ahead and to the right. He waited, concentrating on the spot, wanting to be certain. There was more movement.

"Okay, guys," he said in a stage whisper. "Here we go. Remember the plan. Close the breech and get ready to fire."

He saw a muzzle flash where he'd seen the movement and popped a flare, then scrunched as close to the sandbags as he could and popped a second flare, waiting for the machine-gun burst that would cover his escape from the roof. There was nothing.

"Shoot, you assholes!" he hissed. "Get me the fuck off of here."

"It's broken," the PFC from Scranton whined.

"The fuck it's broken!" Rutkus shouted. "Schmucks! Use your rifles. *Do* something!"

They began firing their rifles, only one on automatic. Rutkus took a deep breath, popped his last flare, and sprang to his left, away from the source of enemy fire, landing on the sloping side of the berm and feeling his ankle roll under him with a sickening chomp. He hobbled into the bunker, slapped the PFC away from the M-60, and righted the ammo belt. Then he slammed the breech shut, pulled the bolt back, and began firing wildly into the field ahead, mad with fright. Down the line, the quad-fifty cut loose, chattering death, ka-death, ka-death, ka-death into the sodden night air. After thirty seconds, the quad stopped firing and Rutkus did, too. There was utter silence. He waited, but whoever was out there had either run away or they'd got him. He waited.

Waited.

Nothing.

It was then that he discovered he'd been hit, nicked in the calf, probably in mid-air as he leapt from the roof of the bunker. Already the blood was squlching in his boot and his leg stung bitterly as his adrenaline surge began to dissipate. As he stared at the growing pool of blood on the wooden floor of the bunker, he felt suddenly embarrassed, as if he'd soiled his mother's carpet in some disgusting way.

"Son of a bitch," he said. "Look at this, willya? Call the Officer of the Guard and tell him I need to go to the aid station."

The PFC from Scranton started to cry and Rutkus told him to shut up or he'd knock his goddamn block off. To the roving guard, he said, "You stay here until somebody comes to relieve you."

The driver from the aid station made him dangle his leg out the door so he wouldn't bleed on the floor of the jeep, and it really began to throb. The medics gave him a shot, unlaced his bloody boot and slipped it off, then gingerly cut his trouser leg away from his wounds, both on his right leg. They hosed it down, scrubbed the wound with antiseptic until it was raw, and stitched it up. Then they wrapped his ankle and sent him back to his hootch.

In the end, when he wrote to his old college roommate about it, the badly sprained ankle was more of a nuisance than his leg, which quickly healed. It could have been worse, of course, and he had to laugh when he compared it to his father's real wound. At least Rutkus was standing his ground and not retreating from a German advance. Then again, he reflected ruefully, a lone Vietnamese sniper is quite a different thing from a Panzer division.

Freedom Bird

SIMMONS sits sixty feet above the ground in the observation tower where Benvenuti, the deranged medic, held Headquarters Company at bay, hurling insults and empty whiskey bottles for two days while they begged him to come down. Finally, he did, spread-eagled, leaping far out from the tower, making the drop in a little over three seconds, bouncing once on the tarmac in the spot they fled to make room for him. And three years earlier, before Simmons was drafted, a staff sergeant from the mess hall went up at night and told the guards they were relieved. Then he set his M-16 on automatic, put the barrel in his mouth, and blew off the top of his head. There are still holes in the roof and they are shown to every new arrival, and all are warned not to do what the sergeant did because it makes a terrible mess that somebody has to clean up.

Simmons is watching for explosions. If he sees any, he has an open frequency to Long Binh and can order helicopters out to see what the trouble is. But it is nearly ten o'clock and there is never any fighting during the day, so Simmons tries to concentrate on the book in his lap, a collection of war stories he took from the USO box in the Orderly Room. He feels sleepy in the sticky heat and has to force himself to look at the pages and stay awake.

A jeep moves toward the compound from the direction of the Plantation and Long Binh, throwing up a huge rooster tail of dust. He knows he is supposed to aim either high or low when shooting at something from a height and is trying to decide which when the jeep pulls into the compound and parks in front of the

Headquarters hootch. Simmons returns to his book and doesn't see the three men emerge from the Orderly Room or the one who points at the tower. The men go back inside and the field phone clatters.

"This is the First Sergeant. Report to the Orderly Room with your gear. I'll send somebody up to relieve you."

"Anything wrong?"

"No. I've got a job for you."

After his relief arrives, Simmons does as he always does when he leaves the tower. He takes a deep breath, looks at the bullet holes in the roof (never look down, he has been told) and swings his leg over the side, reaching frantically with his toe for the first rung. Then he steadies himself and starts down, one rung at a time, his eyes fixed on the holes in the roof. Once, just after he arrived, he did look down. A panic spread through him and he gripped the ladder fiercely and couldn't move. He remained like that for five minutes, halfway between the observation post and the ground, until he talked himself into letting go with his right hand and was able to resume his slow, crab-like descent.

In the Orderly Room, he is greeted by two men wearing Red Cross insignia.

"Have a seat, Robert," one of them says.

"Your father is dead," says the other.

"He didn't suffer," the Red Cross man is saying. "A truck went out of control on the expressway and turned over. He died instantly and painlessly. Emergency leave has been authorized and your commanding officer has granted it."

Simmons sits in a chair by the First Sergeant's desk staring at a spider that has made its web between a filing cabinet and the wall. Outside, high thunderheads roll in from the west as a prelude to the noon rainfall. Simmons wants to kill the spider but is unable to move.

"There will be a few details to clear up, but we'll be

able to get you out of here by eight o'clock tonight. Your First Sergeant will take care of everything. Good-bye, good luck, and I'm sorry." The man extends his hand and Simmons takes it listlessly.

"What should I do?" he says when the Red Cross men have left.

"Pack," says the First Sergeant. "Take everything you want from here because it'll be your last chance."

"Huh?"

"This is it, kid. The war's over for you. When you get home, call your congressman's office and they'll make sure you get reassigned. Climb on that freedom bird tonight and you never have to come back."

Simmons remains in the chair, head bowed, confused.

He spends the afternoon in his hootch, indecisive about what to take home. His plane, an Air Force cargo jet, will take him to Okinawa and he will have to hop a flight from there. The First Sergeant told him to limit himself to fifty pounds, but he doesn't have a scale and fifty pounds doesn't mean anything to him anyway. When he thinks of his father, his chest constricts and he feels abandonded and vulnerable. Members of his unit drop in during the afternoon to say they're sorry and to add: Don't come back. They can't make you come back.

Simmons is thinking that maybe he should come back after the funeral, when things get settled at home. This is too high a price to pay. It should be the other way around—his father greeting the plane carrying Simmons' corpse.

His father was an infantryman in Korea and Simmons has been looking forward to swapping stories with him after he got back. They would go to McGuire's and have supper, just the two of them—his mother would understand—and then, maybe, go to the VFW for drinks. His father liked to tell stories about his war and Simmons has seen enough Koreans in Viet Nam to have an opinion about them. They could compare notes, except that now it will never happen.

"Hey, Simmons," Wilson says, "when you get home, call my girl in Evergreen Park and tell her I'm okay. Sorry about your dad."

Simmons nods. They were in basic training together and went to Fort Polk after that. They are friendly in the way that people who really don't like each other very much are friendly—deliberately and without commitment. Wilson is one of those who will drive him to Bien Hoa. Three of them will take a jeep and be armed to the teeth because it is dangerous to be out after dark. Simmons finishes packing and it occurs to him that he won't have a weapon because he will have to turn in his rifle before he can clear post. Maybe somebody will lend him one.

Before going to the mess hall, he stops to pick up his emergency leave orders and a check for $150 from the Red Cross. The bunker guards for the night are being inspected, and he leans against a shelter and lights a cigarette, watching a lieutenant check rifles and ammunition packs. He can't decide what is more bewildering—the fact that he is going home or his father's death—but he is glad he won't be standing guard tonight. It crosses his mind briefly that the war will continue after he is gone and that men will be wounded and will die, but he doesn't want to think about it. The checker in the mess line wants him to take a malaria pill, but Simmons shows his leave orders and says he isn't going to do it anymore. After supper he goes back to the hootch, drinks a can of beer, and waits.

During the trip to Bien Hoa, he sits in the back of the jeep with his suitcase and other baggage, a borrowed rifle across his lap, tense and frightened. At the airport, his orders are checked and he is told to hurry, that the plane is being boarded now because they want to get out early to avoid an expected rocket attack. Wilson and the other escort unload the jeep and Simmons tells them to be careful on the trip back to the compound.

"Don't forget to call my girl," Wilson says.

Fifteen men, all on emergency leave, stand in line waiting to board the C-135. The plane is still taking on

cargo and Simmons realizes that they are loading caskets. Inside, huge shipping containers are lashed to the
floor with thick webbed straps. The men find folding
seats attached to the inside of the fuselage. Simmons
looks toward the rear but can't see the caskets. He
starts to light a cigarette, but notices a NO SMOKING
sign and keeps the unlit Marlboro between his lips.

The intercom crackles. "This is Major O'Connor,
the pilot. They've got a little shindig planned for us so
we're gonna try to get out of here as soon as we can.
Feel free to smoke once we're aloft. We'll be blacked
out during takeoff. Okay, here we go."

The plane is plunged into blackness when the lights
go out. The engines whine and the big jet rumbles
down the runway, rapidly picking up speed. Simmons,
strapped in his canvas seat, bites on his cigarette and
tries to peer through the dark interior of the plane, half
expecting a Vietnamese rocket to blow him up at any
minute. He feels the plane leave the ground and ascend
rapidly, making a wide, sweeping arc as it rises. The
lights are turned on. "Next stop, Okinawa," Major
O'Connor says. "Smoke 'em if you got 'em."

Simmons lights his cigarette and leans back against
the seat. After he finishes smoking, he stretches out
his legs and falls asleep.

The plane is dark when he awakes, and most of the
men are sleeping. He lights a cigarette and stands to
stretch his legs and allow blood to circulate. He worries that they will have the funeral before he arrives
and decides that they'll wait for him to get home. He
thinks about his mother and can't quite get her face
right in his memory. There is no sense of recognition.
He tries to imagine his father and has better luck until
he begins to picture him in his coffin and the vision
fades. Being in Viet Nam for six months does that to
you, he decides. He thinks about his father's boat.

Ever since Simmons can remember, his father wanted
a boat—nothing elaborate, he always said, just a small
fishing boat. Whenever they went fishing they had to
rent one and his father grumbled about it, saying that

they could go more often if they only had a boat of their own. It was just too damned expensive, though.

Then, one Sunday during the summer before Simmons' sophomore year, a pickup truck stopped in their alley, and his father and the driver unloaded a fifteen-foot lapstrake fishing boat. "Bought it from a guy at McGuire's last night," his father said. "He wanted fifty bucks for it, but I talked him down to forty-five. All it needs is a little work to make it seaworthy."

They leaned it against the garage to inspect it before going out to buy sandpaper and primer and paint. His father tapped the hull with a small mallet and they discovered that half the bottom was ruined by dry rot. "Hell," said his father, "that can be fixed. It'll just take a little longer, that's all." He laughed and laid his hand on his son's shoulder, but Simmons could see the disappointment in his eyes.

The boat stayed there, leaning against the garage, all through high school and the year Simmons spent at the community college. The man who sold it to his father never returned to McGuire's. Now that his father is dead he will get rid of the boat.

"Coming up on Okinawa," the pilot says. "Put your smokes out and buckle up. We've had a change of orders. We'll stop for five hours to refuel and take on cargo, and then continue on to Travis Air Force Base. Anybody that wants to is welcome to ride with us."

In the terminal, Simmons buys himself a milk shake and a small case that has OKINAWA printed on it that hooks onto the strap of his camera and holds an extra roll of film. He also buys cigarettes, candy bars, and snacks to eat on the trip to California.

It is nearly four in the afternoon before they are able to take off. At 1:30, Simmons looked out and saw that the whole plane had been unloaded. When he boards, he looks for the caskets again and can't see them. Before they take off, the pilot tells them they will be arriving just as the sun comes up.

Simmons thinks of one battle story he really wanted to tell his father, about the night they were overrun.

He was in the tower with two other men when the field phone rang. He looked at his watch—it was almost two o'clock. The Sergeant of the Guard wanted to talk to him.

"Take your starlight scope and look over around number four bunker. They think there might be something out there." The sergeant stayed on the line while Simmons focused the scope. As the eerie green landscape came into view, he couldn't believe his eyes. There must have been two companies of Vietnamese just off their south perimeter.

"Gooks everywhere!" he shouted into the field phone. "Holy Jesus, there's a lot of them!"

Then the sirens started and flares went up and small-arms fire crackled in the darkness and a wave of them swept over the compound, knocking down everything in the way. Then they regrouped and washed back again, individuals pausing here and there to shoot at someone or destroy something. Simmons, protected by armor plates on the floor and sides of the tower, saw it all and was unable to do anything about it. He fired his rifle several times and was sure he didn't hit anybody. He and the other men dropped a few grenades, but stopped because they were afraid they'd injure their own men. Bullets slapped against the side of the tower, but he was safe.

Then the Cobras and gunships began to arrive, scudding along the ground below the level of the tower, searchlights on, firing as they came. The noise was deafening. When it was over and the Vietnamese had melted back into the forest, Simmons came down, eyes fixed on the holes in the roof, and smelled the acrid smell of gunpowder and heard the moaning of the wounded men. He helped where he could and when the awards came out he received an Army Commendation Medal for alerting the compound.

Simmons wakes at five o'clock and knows they will be landing soon. He thinks about going back, retaining a vague notion that that is the proper thing to do. He thinks of spiders and snakes and the jungle rot on his feet and in his crotch. He thinks of the fierce heat and helicopters and artillery and centipedes. Of Vietnamese whores and of corpses lying on their backs after battle. Rats as big as small dogs and the certainty of death. He thinks of all these things and knows he will not return to Viet Nam.

It is all backwards, he tells himself. His father should be alive and grieving. But that isn't the way it has turned out and he will have to live with it.

He is certain of nothing but loss.

The sun is beginning to rise as the plane approaches the coast. From Simmons' small window, the land mass looks very black and he can see patterns made by street lights. Over the mountains the sky is orange. Men begin waking to the realization that they are almost home, but there is no rejoicing on the plane.

"We're over California," Major O'Connor says over the intercom. "We'll be landing in approximately ten minutes. Have anything you want to declare ready for customs inspection. Fasten your seat belts, and welcome home, men."

Simmons lights a final cigarette, closes his eyes, and waits, then feels the plane rise slightly beneath him and bank left to begin the long, slow descent into the bright dawn, the bitterness, the regret.

The Recurrent Dream Hold

RICHARD Terry stirs at the sound of his alarm clock, groans, rolls over and prepares to face another day at the Shell station. He works three days a week but would rather work nights, as he prefers the semi-solitude, quiet mornings, and the sunrise over the cornfield across the highway. His back hurts again today and he blames it on the weather. Too fucking damp, he mutters. He is awake now.

Everyone else in the house is asleep, the previous night's drunkenness waning by degrees. When they rise they will be ready for another daylong search for diversion. Richard would like to be with them, but his unemployment checks aren't enough to support a constant revel. All the men living in the house work part time at the Shell station. Richard's hours go on somebody else's check so the people at the unemployment office won't know he's earning money. When they're not working they sit on the porch drinking and smoking and making jokes about the world as it passes by.

"Next? What can I do for you?" says the clerk at the unemployment office.

"I got out of the Army three weeks ago."

"What do you want with us?"

"I'm going back to school in the fall. They told me I could get unemployment benefits."

"You a student? You can't file a claim against a school."

"I know."

"You'll have to file against the Army. What did you do?"

"Infantry."

"A grunt, eh? Kill many gooks?"

"No. I . . ."

"Well, look, you're in the wrong office. Go down the hall and come back here when they let you go. We'll get you something." The clerk has a superior tone in his voice, as if he were doing Richard a favor. Thinking he has been made to look foolish he turns and quickly leaves the office, feeling like a vagrant.

"Fill it with premium. And check the oil," the man orders, and Richard nods, a pump jockey. When he's at work he becomes a gas station attendant, his anger muted by occupation. He wears jungle boots and a COAT, MAN'S, COTTON W/R RIP STOP, POPLIN FOR TROPICAL WEAR. A patch on his shoulder once identified him as a member of the 196th Light Infantry Brigade.

The driver sits impassively as Richard opens the hood to check the oil, the gas pump running automatically. The man is balding, and heavy loose flesh hangs over the collar of his white shirt. His arms are ineffectually stuffed into short sleeves, and a plastic pen holder identifies him as a representative of the Acme Lumber Company. He lights a cigarette and coughs, a high rasping cough that annoys Richard under the hood. "Your oil's okay," he calls, slamming the hood.

"You over in Nam?" The assumed familiarity annoys him. Richard never says "Nam."

"Yes."

"What's it like over there? I heard it's rough."

"Sometimes it is and sometimes it isn't."

"Get the windshield, huh? Yeah, I was in the service during Korea. I didn't get over, mind you. We wouldn't have this trouble now if they let MacArthur go into China like he wanted. The Chinese are behind all this, you know." He sticks his head out the window so Richard can hear.

"I didn't see any Chinese."

"They're behind it, all right. Them and those Russians. I say we should've bombed 'em to hell and be done with it."

"Three-fifty," Richard says. "You save stamps?" He

accepts the company credit card in exchange for two pages of yellow gift stamps.

When there are no customers he sits on a bench in front of the station and listens to the traffic on the interstate and watches the corn across the highway. Sometimes he reads. One of the Red Cross girls had given him a copy of *Cat's Cradle* when he was in the hospital and now he reads anything by Kurt Vonnegut that falls into his hands. He rarely reads the papers, preferring to glance at the headlines and learn what he can from that.

After he was wounded they gave him a desk job, promoted him to Sergeant, and awarded him a Purple Heart and an Army Commendation Medal. His company commander requested a Bronze Star, but the battalion sent it back. It didn't matter much anyway. What he wanted was to go home. They also took him off guard duty, but that was after he wrote to his congressman. When he couldn't sleep nights he would get dressed and walk around the compound, chatting with the guards in the bunkers. They couldn't do much about his wanderings without risking an investigation of some sort so they left him alone. Often during the day he could be seen at the compound's swimming pool, paddling around on an inner tube, his back invisible beneath the surface of the water.

He doesn't mind working at the gas station. In the fall he'll start his final year of school and will complete his degree in business administration. He hopes the degree and his war record will be enough to get him a good job. If not, he will use the GI Bill to get a master's degree in something. Sometimes he says he wants to go to law school. His plans aren't definite.

"Have you had any gainful employment in the past two weeks?" says the clerk.

"No."

"You know, Mr. Terry, we have ways of finding out

if somebody's lying to us. If you're working we'll find out about it sooner or later. We have our ways."

"I answered your question. Can I have my check?"

The clerk hands him the check for $106. It must be endorsed twice, once here and again at the bank. Richard signs his name and returns the pen to the clerk, ensconced behind a long gray counter. "You GIs think you're pretty smart, don't you? I'm going to make sure you don't draw unemployment and the GI Bill at the same time. I've put a hold on your checks for the middle of September. What do you think of that?"

"See you in two weeks," says Richard.

At the bank a middle-aged woman eyes him and accepts the check. "A strong boy like you—," she says and hands him the money.

The night he was wounded, his platoon set up an ambush where a jungle path made a right-angle turn. In the briefing room they had been told the path was a supply route for the Viet Cong unit operating in the area.

"Supplies have been moving along this trail for quite some time now," the Sergeant Major said. "Our Intelligence reports that they're going to the 48th Sapper Battalion. We're going to block the path and interdict the supply route." As he said this he made an X with his index finger on the wall map.

Some of the men snorted. The 48th Sapper Battalion was held responsible for everything that went wrong in their area. Hardly a day went by when they weren't blamed for something. A broken phone wire, a hole in the road, an unexpected explosion: all were taken as evidence of their activity. The unit was real enough and had caused a lot of trouble during the Tet offensive, but that was long before any of these men had arrived, and they had never seen the sapper group. Terry chuckled with the others.

It wasn't quite dark when the big Chinook set down and the men scrambled out the side door, leaping five

feet to the ground and spreading out around the helicopter until it rose and scooted off to deposit another
squad a few miles farther on. The men moved a half
mile down the path and a few yards into the jungle to
hide for an hour, and then moved to the ambush site,
another mile down the path. They had a new lieutenant with them, a transfer from the 1st Division.

When it was dark, and the civilians were home
where they belonged, they set up their ambush at the
wide part of the bend. They had two M-60 machine
guns and aimed them down the legs of the path. In the
middle they set up a starlight scope on a swivel. Behind
the scope sat Lieutenant Higa and the radio man. The
men broke into fire teams and situated themselves
around the machine guns, a few yards into the jungle.

Richard Terry took his flak jacket off and laid it
across a log, tilted his helmet back on his neck and,
rifle across his lap, waited for sunrise. He didn't like to
be out at night and felt that theirs was a futile assign-
ment. Nothing ever happened on these ambushes. In
the night heat the insect repellent mixed with sweat
and ran into his eyes, stinging and adding to his dis-
comfort. Some of the others slapped at bugs and kept
an eye out for snakes. Terry began to doze.

A noise alerted him, and he watched a water buffalo
loom into view and lumber along the path, accompanied by a drunk peasant who sang songs and slapped at
it with a willow switch. The duo passed around the
bend, oblivious of the group of armed men hidden in
the forest, any one of whom could have reached out
from his hiding place and sent the man sprawling in
the dust with a well-placed kick.

Terry dozed again, head tipped back.

"Live grenade!" somebody hissed, and they all lay
close to the earth, trying to become part of it, desperate
for shelter until the muffled thud sent thousands of
steel fragments whizzing through the foliage. At Long
Binh they said it was good for Terry that his head was
tilted back, as the steel helmet protected his neck from
the flying bits of metal.

Private First Class Stafford, who had thrown the grenade into the forest, repeated that it was an accident; that he didn't mean to do it; it was a mistake. Terry lay on his stomach and screamed at Stafford. "You son of a bitch! I'll kill you. God damn you. Where's my rifle? I'll kill the fucker. Bastard. Goddamn fucker," while the medic examined his wounds and injected morphine into him to quiet him down.

Holding the radio receiver between his chin and shoulder, Lieutenant Higa droned, "Red Man, this is Charles Francis," calmly, as if he were calling a taxi. "We've taken fire. I need a dust-off for one man. Shrapnel. You know our position. Over." Then he told his platoon to empty their weapons into the forest. For three weeks Terry thought there really had been a fight. Four other men received slight wounds. Terry was in the hospital at Zama, Japan, for six weeks, and when he returned, Stafford had been transferred to another battalion.

After getting off work, he showers, shaves, and puts on clean clothes. Then he discovers a note telling him that everybody else is at Mac's, a neighborhood bar, and that he should come over. Instead, he gets a beer from the refrigerator and stations himself on the front porch. It's hot and he props his feet on the railing and sips his beer slowly. He decides he'll go to Mac's after the news is on.

He is excited by the sound of gunfire, watching, fascinated, as a helicopter skims the tops of trees, fifty-calibre machine guns rattling away at invisible targets. He scans the television soldiers for a familiar face and opens another can of beer. He snaps the set off after the news and returns to the porch with the evening paper.

When he returned from Japan, Captain Jenkins wanted to send him home, but the battalion commander said he should find something for Terry to do. A man with three years of college can be valuable in an orderly room. Make him work. The doctors say he's fit for duty; it will do him good. "Not favorably considered."

"I'm sorry, Richard," Jenkins told him. "Colonel Harwick turned your application down. I'll see what I can find you in the Orderly Room."

Terry walked away, fighting tears of frustration in the steamy heat until he was sure no one would see him. Sitting in an empty guard bunker, he surveyed the desolation around the compound. All about him the closely cropped and cratered earth stretched far away, and he thought of the remaining five months he had to spend doing nothing and counting days.

He scans the headlines as usual, and drops the paper on the floor. He has a copy of *The Sirens of Titan* and he begins to read. The beer is working in him, though, and he soon loses interest in the book. He sits on the porch staring blankly toward the street, the half-empty can of beer warming in his lap.

"Sergeant Terry. Get a jeep and a driver and take these papers to the mortuary at Ton Son Nhut. Alfred over at Personnel has your authorization."

"Yes, Sir."

"Another thing. Stop by the PX and get some film for my camera. Slide film."

"Okay."

The waiting wasn't as difficult as he thought it would be. His days were spent reading in the Orderly Room or running errands for Captain Jenkins, who seemed to feel he had let Terry down. He was seldom asked to perform his normal military duties. When his back hurt, the medics gave him drugs to stop the pain. He spent a lot of time at the pool and, in a way, felt freer than ever before in his life.

Two men had been killed the night before and their personnel files had to be shipped back with the bodies. Terry didn't know the men, both Privates, and in fact didn't think about them at all. Inwardly content, he strapped a pistol around his waist and prepared to set off for the airbase on the other side of Saigon. The paper Sergeant Alfred gave him authorized him "to deliver documents at Ton Son Nhut Airbase," and he swelled with a sense of his own importance. The open jeep speeding along the dusty road south provided a respite from the heat, and Terry smoked cigarettes, helmet tipped back, and blew smoke over his shoulder.

The mortuary itself was surrounded by a twelve-foot-high plywood fence. A large, prominent sign was nailed to the fence near the entranceway.

ATTENTION: THIS IS A PLACE OF DEATH. ARMY REGULATIONS FORBID THE PRESENCE OF CAMERAS AND UNAUTHORIZED PERSONNEL. YOU WILL CONDUCT YOURSELF WITH APPROPRIATE DIGNITY WITHIN THESE PREMISES.

Inside the sanctuary a semiformal garden stretched along the wall and a cloistered walk reached toward a shady arena. He was greeted by an attendant in a light green tunic who beckoned to him. "This way, please." A sweet, artificial stench bore down upon him as they passed row after row of refrigerated shelves. Turning a corner behind his guide he caught a glimpse of stacked aluminum caskets, petitioners at the rear of a shrine.

In the workroom, a row of stainless steel tables was illuminated by fluorescent tubes. A partially reconstructed skeleton lay on one of the tables, the bones charred and broken. The skull had been crushed and the jaw was missing. A pile of rubberized cloth bags lay in a corner, a brownish trickle hardening beneath them. In another corner, filing cabinets had been arranged to form a sort of office. Shiny metal insignia identified the cherub-faced man at the desk as a captain in the medical corps.

"Yes, Sergeant. What can I do for you?" Terry felt a tightening in his stomach and made small circles with his hand on one of the filing cabinets.

"I ... I'm from the one-ninety-sixth," he stammered. "Light infantry. I brought these." He held the records out.

"Ah, yes," said the captain. "They're all ready to go,

except for these." He made some notes in a ledger on his desk. "Did you know them?"

"No," Terry hesitated. "They were new. Only been here a little while. What's that?" He pointed to the skeleton.

"We don't know. They're trying to get a dental trace on him. He's been here ten days now and we'd like to send him home, but we have to have positive identification. It's a shame when they come in like that." Terry stared at the Captain. Safe in his cell, he never saw the fighting, only its mangled and mutilated sequel.

"I have to be back before dark."

"Yes. Specialist Fenlon will show you out. Nice talking to you."

Shading his eyes in the bright tropical sun outside the mortuary, Terry found his driver asleep and shook him awake. On the runway a huge transport plane was accepting oblong metal boxes into its belly. Terry watched until he couldn't see them anymore, feeling suddenly old and tired.

It's almost dark. A motorcycle jolts Richard from his reverie. In the fading light he spills warm beer onto the lawn, watching with satisfaction as it seeps into the dirt. He wishes there was something exciting to do, anything to relieve his stifling boredom. There is a faint glow about the city and he remembers awful silences when flares hung in the sky, their eerie light revealing unearthly, pockmarked landscapes. And helicopters belched bullets in the night, every fifth one a tracer, firing so fast it looked as though red cords anchored them to the ground. That, anyway, was exciting, and he feels a vague sense of loss, wanting but not wanting.

During his last ten days he did nothing but lie around the pool, drink beer, and play cards. His baggage had been shipped home and he was relieved of all duties. The night before he left, he went to the NCO club and stayed until closing. Then he took a bottle of bourbon and made the rounds of the bunkers.

Next morning, travel orders in hand, he was driven to Long Binh and deposited unceremoniously at the gate of the 90th Replacement Battalion. The jeep disappeared down the road, heading back toward the compound. He stood in the road watching where the jeep had been until the dust settled. Then he turned and presented a copy of his travel orders to the guard, who directed him toward the outprocessing center. Once inside, he began his outprocessing by passing through a shabby plywood archway. Overhead a large scroll was emblazoned with a sign, WELCOME TO THE WORLD, crudely lettered in red and blue paint.

Grote Apart

I

QUITE unexpectedly, and after nearly fifteen years, Timothy Grote has begun to imagine that he performed heroic acts in Viet Nam. He does this at night, after his wife has gone to bed, when he sits with his headphones on in his brown fake-leather chair, drinking beer and listening to the music he listened to then: the Beatles, Supremes, Four Tops, Cream, Iron Butterfly, Moody Blues. Sometimes he falls asleep and knocks his can of beer to the floor. When he does that, he wakes with a start, curses, and, clumsy with sleep, stumbles to the kitchen for paper towels to sop up the mess, hoping that his wife won't notice. She does, of course, and reproaches him with baleful looks on mornings following his reminiscences.

What he is trying to do is to make sense out of what happened, or didn't happen, to him in the war in Southeast Asia. What didn't happen was this: nobody shot him or stabbed him with a bayonet or threw hand grenades or shot rockets at him. Nor did he shoot, bayonet, grenade, or rocket anybody else. No snakes, rats, centipedes, or panthers bit him. He didn't take drugs. He wasn't disobedient. He didn't get very many medals.

The things that did happen when he was in Viet Nam are far less interesting than the things that might have happened. He worked in an artillery-battalion Personnel Office, stood guard duty every third night, and got drunk on most of the other nights. He played poker and won more than he lost. He tried to learn photography but gave it up in disgust when the pictures wouldn't come out right. He and his roommate stole materials from the Quartermaster Sergeant and fixed up their room in the Personnel hootch. He borrowed books from the USO library and didn't give them back. His girlfriend stopped writing to him.

When he gets drunk at night, he pores over his memories, like a clutter of old photographs, searching for something noteworthy. When he finds something, he examines it in detail, looking at it from every angle, studying all its facets until he satisfies himself that it is unimportant. Like the time the south perimeter was fired upon, one of the few times anybody on the compound had the opportunity to be shot.

Grote was on guard duty on the north side of the compound, a fourteen-acre tract of land located thirty miles north of Saigon and owned, through some remarkable swindle, by Trans-Pacific Architects and Engineers, an American defense-contracting firm. It was surrounded by an eight-foot-high ridge of dirt into which the bunkers had been built, like peculiar decorations on a Bundt cake. Surrounding the berm was a row of treacherous concertina wire in high, looping coils. Next came the minefield (where Grote went once, as part of a detail assigned to pick up beer cans thrown away by the guards during the night), and finally the outer fence, topped by more concertina wire. At 1:30 the field phone clattered; it was the Officer of the Guard, warning everybody that something seemed suspicious on the south perimeter. That was enough for Grote, who put his flak jacket on, grabbed his rifle, and started for the door.

"Get your ass back in here, shithead," the Sergeant in charge said.

Thinking about it now, Grote squirms in his chair. Afterwards, they heard what might have been three rifle shots, and the whole south perimeter cut loose in retaliation, sounding like some great roaring beast: rifles, machine guns, and grenade launchers firing like mad for thirty seconds. The following morning, when a reconnaissance patrol went out to look around, there were no corpses and they couldn't find any spent shell casings. Still, the men on the south perimeter swore they saw muzzle flashes and heard the bullets whizzing overhead.

Not much in the way of heroism there, Grote has to admit. Yet he pursues it, recreating the entire sequence, searching for the kernel of dignity that might be there. The Sergeant misunderstood, of course. Grote's intention was to go and help out on the south side, not to run to the bomb shelters, which were airless and smelly and chock-full of snakes and spiders and other obnoxious creatures. He tried to explain, but the Sergeant cut him off.

"Who the fuck is going to protect this perimeter if everybody's over on the other side of the compound?"

The Sergeant was right and Grote knew it at the time. If you do a dumb thing, Grote now knows, people don't remember that your intentions were good. All they remember is that you did a dumb thing, like waving at an ambush patrol in a helicopter.

Three times during his eight months in Viet Nam, Grote was named Clerk of the Week. Mister Binks, the warrant officer in charge of the Personnel Section, reasoned that recognizing one of his clerks each week would improve everybody's efficiency and morale. The Clerk of the Week got a half day off and a cardboard plaque that sat on his desk until the next Clerk of the Week was selected. Grote spent his free afternoon at the NCO club drinking gin and tonic while watching black-and-white reruns of *I Love Lucy* and *Leave It to Beaver* on the fancy Panasonic color television at the end of the bar. He decided to have a swim before supper.

The swimming pool was a mystery to Grote. Nobody on the compound really knew how the battalion's proudest possession came into being. The version Grote opted for featured the Battalion Sergeant Major, a Corps of Engineers excavation squad waylaid on its way to Firebase Bearcat, seven quarts of whiskey, seven

Vietnamese whores, seven T-bone steaks, and a rubber-and-canvas helicopter landing pad that the Quarter-master Sergeant had acquired by devious means. It even had a lifeguard, a PFC unaccountably drafted out of Grosse Pointe, Michigan, who spent his days skimming bugs off the surface of the water, keeping the railroad ties that secured the landing pad in place, and maintaining the crude filtering system.

Grote was floating on an inner tube, reading *Johnny Got His Gun* (approved by the Battalion Censor because it was a war story "of some kind"), when the Chinook carrying the ambush patrol passed overhead. Grote glanced up from his book and waved at the door gunner, who responded by lazily extending his middle finger. Grote misunderstood and waved harder and before he realized what was happening the helicopter stopped, backed up, and hovered over the swimming pool while three infantrymen leaned out the door and tried to piss on him.

When Grote surfaced, still clutching his ruined book, one of the infantrymen shouted at him, "Get fucked, wimp!" Fifteen years later, Grote can still hear the words echoing in his mind's ear and feels his face getting hot as he scrunches deeper into his wing chair, moodily sipping his beer. From the point of view of the men in the helicopter, what they did wasn't so bad. The blast from the rotors blew the urine away. At the time they were going out to spend a week in the boonies and get shot at, while the guy in the swimming pool would be sitting on his ass at a desk all day and drinking beer at night. Besides, anybody who could afford to spend the afternoon in a swimming pool fifteen miles from Long Binh probably deserved to be pissed on.

From Grote's point of view it was altogether different. He waved in a spirit of comradeship, the feeling that men who bear arms and wear the same uniform are supposed to have for each other. It wasn't his fault that he was a Personnel clerk and they were infantrymen. They probably would have liked to be Personnel clerks too, so they wouldn't have to go out in the woods to be blown up or shot. He wonders if things like that happened in World War II and Korea. He supposes they did, but that was different. His generation got stuck with a bum war.

None of it made sense. For eight months he sat at the same desk in the Personnel Section, processing men into the battalion, then assigning them to one of the four artillery batteries, the machine-gun battery, the searchlight battery, or, if they were lucky, to Headquarters Battery. After that, he never knew what happened to them unless they were killed or wounded. Ned Swenson, his roomate in the Personnel hootch, kept track of casualties.

Grote struggles to his feet and makes his way unsteadily to the stereo to turn up the volume, the better to hear one of his favorite songs. Every night in Viet Nam, when they didn't have guard duty, he and Swenson ended their drinking session by playing *The Four Tops' Greatest Hits* on Swenson's tape player. After "Shake Me, Wake Me, When It's Over," the last song, they would stumble outside to urinate in the ditch that ran behind the hootch, then return to their room to fall onto their beds where fans blew the sodden tropical air over them for what remained of the night. Grote concentrates on the song, the hard-driving Motown beat sending him back in his imagination.

That's what it was, they agreed every night, a yearlong dream, a seemingly endless succession of absurd and paradoxical images. A crash course in ennui. For the men in combat units it was a nightmare, far worse than anything Grote can imagine, and he sometimes feels apologetic when he talks to a former tanker or infantryman, especially if they know he spent his time in the comparative safety of a battalion base camp. Still, he *was* there, and there was always the chance that somebody would shoot him. It's not his fault that nobody did. He still thinks he earned his hazardous-duty pay. There were other dangers: spiders, snakes, centipedes, rats.

Rats. The mere thought of them fills him with loathing. Keld, the PFC who lived in the room next to his, awoke one night to find one of them perched on the foot of his bed and began shrieking and kicking at it, waking up the entire hootch. When they got to his room the rat was gone, but Keld had a cut on his foot. Even though he swore that he scratched it on the metal bed frame and that the rat never touched him, he was ordered to undergo the painful rabies series. Shortly afterwards, the Rat Assassins began their vendetta.

Grote was brushing his teeth by the spigot that extended upward from the pipe paralleling the ditch behind the hootch when he first became aware of the Rat Assassins. He perceived movement of some kind at the edge of his peripheral vision, and when he turned he saw a two-foot-high flame dancing to and fro in what appeared to be a metal box. Toothbrush in hand, he approached the three men, Keld and his two roommates, who were staring with satisfaction at the flame, which paused at one end of the box, lurched spasmodically, then remained stationary. The box turned out to be an animal trap, the kind gardeners use when they want to catch rabbits and other pests but don't want to hurt them, with doors that drop shut at the ends to trap the animal when it takes the bait. The rat had been caught during the night, then doused with kerosene and set on fire in the morning. Grote studied the smoldering rodent for a moment, then glanced at Keld and his assistants, then returned to the ditch to finish brushing his teeth. Some heroes.

At 2:30, Grote is getting drowsy, but he has half a can of Budweiser left and his song isn't over yet. The Four Tops' lead singer is whining into the finale, but Grote doesn't hear the end of the song, nor does he hear the record going shhtkk . . . shhtkk . . . shhtkk for ten minutes. Suddenly, he jerks awake, swings his hand away from his body, and sends what remains of his beer sprawling across the hardwood floor toward the Oriental rug he and his wife argued about before eventually buying. He scrambles to protect the carpet, sweeping the beer back with his cupped hand. When the puddle seems stable, he rises and hurries to the kitchen for paper towels, wondering what revenge his wife has in store for him this time. Had the beer reached the carpet, he is quite certain, she'd stab him in the heart with an ice pick.

When the floor is clean, he carries the beer-smelly paper towels out to the garbage can, hoping to hide the evidence from his wife. It is nearly three o'clock, but he doesn't have any classes until the following afternoon. He pours himself a short glass of wine from the jug in the refrigerator, then returns to his chair in the corner to listen to the Four Tops again, wondering halfway through the song why he isn't capable of making his wife understand and whether it's ever going to be over.

II

By the time he drags himself out of bed and shuffles to the bathroom, Grote's wife has been at work two hours already. He is never aware of her leaving, as she is a master of stealth in the morning, slipping silently from between the sheets and padding softly to the bedroom door, which she closes noiselessly behind her. She always lays her clothes out on the dining room table before going to bed, so there is no need for her to return to the bedroom once she's effected her escape. Her pajamas and robe she rolls into a tight, neat bundle that she stashes on a shelf in the bathroom along with her slippers. Mouth foaming with toothpaste, Grote has an impulse to unroll and repack the bundle in an eccentric way, just to see what she'll do when she discovers the change. She'd notice, of course.

She knows everything about him: how many cans of beer he drinks each night, how many cigarettes he smokes, whether or not he stops off for a beer at Fogarty's after his night class, if he's been drinking bourbon at the Cork and Bottle. He doesn't know how she knows, but he sometimes thinks that her only interest in life, aside from her job at the Campus Counseling Center, is keeping track of his dissipations. He rinses his mouth and toothbrush, having decided to shave and shower after he has his morning coffee and cigarette.

There is no coffee for him in the kitchen. Instead, he finds the electric percolator inverted in the dish drainer, along with her coffee mug and one spoon. It wasn't that way last night: when he went to bed it was sitting upright, the pot full of water and the basket full of coffee to make eight cups. She normally has two and leaves the remainder for him, as he doesn't mind drinking three-hour-old coffee. He is certain she didn't drink the whole pot, because caffeine makes her jumpy at work. Why throw out six cups of serviceable, if somewhat stale, coffee, he wonders. He fills the percolator with water, inserts the shaft and slips the basket over it, then opens the freezer, where his wet fingers stick momentarily to the three-pound can of Folgers. Inside the coffee can is an envelope with his name written in her tight, perfect handwriting. *Timothy.* She always calls him Timothy when she means business.

The percolator (expensive Chilton—wedding present from Sheilagh's dissertation adviser) gurgling cheerfully, Timothy Grote perches on his stool at the breakfast bar, smoking a cigarette and reading the note his wife left him:

Timothy,

It was three-thirty when you finally came to bed last night. You drank nine and a half (I saw the mess you made on the floor. You can't fool me, Timothy) cans of beer and the equivalent of half a bottle of wine. You smoked a pack and a half of cigarettes while you sat in the corner listening to your stupid music and drinking yourself into a coma. Then you came reeling into our bedroom (it's *my* bedroom, too, don't forget that) stinking like a brewery. On top of that, you snored like a pig and I didn't get any sleep for the

rest of the night. THIS CANNOT CONTINUE.
Do you understand?

Now pay attention. After your class this afternoon, I want you to come straight home—no stopping off at Fogarty's for a beer, no Cork and Bottle, nothing. STRAIGHT HOME. We need to talk. You are ruining your health and making me a nervous wreck. I do not know how much longer I can endure this, but I do not intend to spend the rest of my life watching you make a mess of yours.

S.

P.S. From now on, you can make your own fucking coffee.

"Damn it, Sheilagh," he says.

He imagines her now, sitting in her comfortable office in the counseling center, leaning back reflectively, perhaps with her fingertips pressed together, probably with a fresh Number 2 pencil stuck through her red hair over her right ear. ("It gives me an air of amiable authority. That's important to a therapist.") Sunlight streaming in from the window behind her makes her hair luminous, radiant, and it also hides her features in shadow so that her facial expressions will not betray her. ("What I think is not important; what is important is that I help my clients with their problems and get them to a better place.") The victim is seated in another comfortable chair discreetly dabbing at her eyes with a tissue she's snatched from the box placed discreetly on the low, glass-topped table next to her. ("It's important that they cry; we have to get in touch with their real emotions and feelings.") Five minutes before the end of the session, Sheilagh will glance at her watch and say, "Now I think it's time for us to gather in all we've accomplished today."

Grote pours himself some coffee and lights another cigarette, wondering what she intends to accomplish with him. Wouldn't it be nice, he muses, if he came home to find her waiting in bed, with champagne and bread and cheese laid out on the night stand, and they would frolic the afternoon away, then go out for a nice meal downtown? He thinks of her red pubic hair and smooth thighs, her body supple and lithe at thirty-six, and feels a slight tremor in his crotch. No way, he thinks; not with the tone of that note. Besides, that isn't her style. Her *modus operandi* is altogether different. "If you know what's going to happen," she told him once, "it loses something. I want it to be mysterious, exciting." Sheilagh relies on the element of surprise.

Their lovemaking, when it occurs, nearly always follows her initiative. She might stop him in the short hallway between the two downstairs bedrooms and without saying anything begin grinding herself against his thigh. Or, after dinner, before he's had too much to drink, she'll come around to his side of the table to rub his shoulders, then will lean down and swiftly dart her tongue into his ear. Occasionally, usually on a weekend, she'll climb into the shower with him and they'll do it standing, being careful not to slip and fall down. Rarely, and then usually after a party when he's been particularly witty and charming, is Sheilagh interested in sex at night. "It's the alcohol," she complains. "It's a depressant. Jesus, I don't have all night, you know."

Then, about a year and a half ago, Sheilagh began developing strange habits. She stopped smoking, for one thing, and reduced her alcohol consumption to a mere trickle. She staked out the extra downstairs bedroom as her own and effectively barred Grote from going in there, though she did allow him to paint it for her, a pale, deathly white, and had him install brackets for bookshelves. She bought a navy-blue carpet and matching floor-length drapes. In the end, she made everything in the room either navy or white: the bullet lamps and desk accessories are blue, as is the occasional chair she found on sale at the shopping mall. The severe desk and matching chair, hideous Danish things she fell in love with at the Modern Furniture Mart, are white. The walls of her study, as she now calls it, are decorated with garish Marimekko prints, the cheap cloth stretched over wooden frames. When she goes in there and shuts the door behind her, it's as if she passes out of his life altogether.

The rest of the house, furnished with odds and ends and things he inherited from his parents, stuff that Sheilagh calls the dead people's furniture, contrasts sharply with her study, which is relentlessly tidy. She vacuums her room every third day, but generally lets the rest of the house go unless they're having dinner guests or a party, though they haven't been entertaining much for the last year. The living room, which Grote loves and Sheilagh hates, contains his parents' Duncan-Phyfe sofa, reupholstered in a subtle blue and green brocade; two chairs that had been his grandparents'; his mother's rocking chair; an octagonal table on which his chess set, dusty and unused, sits next to a ginger-jar lamp; a carved oak tea table; his wing chair; her red velvet wing chair, which she rarely uses anymore; and the carpet they fought about.

A deep, cerulean blue with a pink and green floral border that is echoed in the medallion, it would be perfect with their other furniture, Sheilagh insisted. When Grote protested that it was too expensive, she countered that, for Christ's sake, we're both working, and he relented. Now that she's shifted into her Danish-modern mode, Sheilagh has become utterly indifferent to the carpet, while Timothy, at night when he is alone with a small fire in the fireplace and the only other light supplied by a double-globe brass lamp on the mantel, has begun finding it mysterious and lovely. Sheilagh says it reminds her of a funeral parlor.

Something peculiar is going on with his wife, something that Grote can't understand. For the last eight months, it seems, she's been avoiding him. No more humping in the shower, and during their infrequent lovemaking she just lies there, staring over his shoulder at the ceiling. For all her enthusiasm, she might as well be reading the newspaper or listening to one of her young clients unburden herself of her despair over not making the cheerleading squad. She's also developed the curious habit of sneaking off to bed without telling him, slipping unobtrusively down the hall between the two bedrooms and leaving both doors closed so he won't know which room she's in. She dresses herself in gaudy, frumpy clothes around the house and smears Noxema over her face at night, making her smell like the aftermath of a long day at the beach. No more tricks like wrapping herself in a satin sheet in front of the fire and beckoning him to come to her. Sometimes, he worries that she's having an affair; other times he wishes she would. Maybe she'd get it out of her system and conclude that he's a pretty good deal, after all.

Another thing she's done to annoy him lately is to become a vegetarian, so that when it's his turn to cook, he has to prepare two different meals. What he generally does is make a pot of macaroni and cheese or some kind of vegetarian casserole and a salad, then grill himself a pork chop or small steak. When it's her turn she gives no quarter, and the odors of tofu, brown rice, coconut oil, frying peppers and other things that give him heartburn assail him as he makes his way up the walk from the garage to the house. The refrigerator is crammed with things that look like they belong in a chemistry lab. The one who doesn't cook has to wash the dishes and her mess is always twice as bad as his, and since she refuses to wash dishes that have had meat on them, he ends up doing three-fourths of the dishes anyway.

Grote simply can't imagine what's come over her, or what he's done to offend her. Aside from brooding about Viet Nam and worrying about whether he'll be awarded tenure, he can't think of any annoying things he does. He does the grocery shopping and his share of the housework, as well as his own laundry. He does the yard work and she tends the garden, which is rarely productive. There is, of course, his drinking.

To his way of thinking, it isn't a problem except on those nights when an imp gets into him and he sits up reliving his time in Southeast Asia. When that happens, the alcohol comforts him, dulling his senses so that he can tolerate the reality that he can't otherwise face, namely, that he was disposable. Not in the sense that all soldiers are disposable—Grote accepted that by the time he was halfway through basic training—but that his draft board, acting on behalf of his fellow citizens, had plucked him out of graduate school and handed him over to the Army, saying in effect, "Here, take this one. He's no good to us. Do what you like with him." And it's not that Grote thought he deserved special treatment—nobody should have gone to Viet Nam.

He knows that he drinks too much when he thinks about it, also that if he doesn't drink himself into a stupor he won't be able to sleep at all. It happens less often in winter. However, when it starts getting hot in late spring, something in his body chemistry responds and he finds himself thinking about the war and drinking by himself late at night. If he thinks about it hard enough, if he can turn it around in his mind until he finds the clue to what's bothering him, maybe he can free himself from this thing that gnaws at him like a weasel. It is also when the weather's hot that his dream recurs.

It is always the same: Grote is walking, naked and weaponless, on a sandy berm. He knows he is in Viet Nam, having been called back even though he finished his tour of duty. The fact that they haven't given him a uniform or rifle puzzles him every time. It is daylight, but there are flares popping all around and floating down on little parachutes like the ones he used to make out of his father's handkerchiefs when he was a boy. There is a sense of urgency, and, terror building within him, he begins to walk faster toward the blockhouse that sits in the middle of the berm, his feet burning on the hot sand. Parallel coils of concertina wire lie on both sides of the berm, looping lazily toward the blockhouse, their razor-sharp edges capable of slashing him to shreds, should he trip and fall into them. Something terrible is in the blockhouse, yet he hurries toward it. It is at this point that he begins to howl, a low, guttural moan that becomes more high-pitched as its intensity increases. He begins running, hearing himself moan through his sleep. The blockhouse recedes from him and he runs faster, somehow quite conscious of the fact that he is now bellowing like a trapped animal, until he sprawls in the hot sand and begins rolling down the incline into the concertina wire, which he knows will kill him. At this point, he wakes up.

Usually, Sheilagh is pounding him on his sweaty back and yelling at him that he's been dreaming and that he should wake up and then go back to sleep again, which is the rational way of dealing with this sort of thing.

"I was in Viet Nam again," he says, almost whimpering.

At first she was sympathetic, and would hold him against her breast and stroke his head. A couple of times, she raised her nightgown and pulled him over on top of her to comfort him that way, but she grew tired of it and began attributing the dream to his drinking.

"If you didn't sit up until all hours getting drunk and thinking about it, maybe you wouldn't have that dream," she said the last time it happened, then rolled over on her side away from him, and Grote folded his arms across his chest and stared at the ceiling until daybreak.

III

Her car, the snappy blue Honda Accord, is safely ensconced in the garage when he gets home, and he parks his green Volkswagen directly behind it, unconcerned about blocking her in because he's half-decided to go to the Cork and Bottle later on. If he doesn't go out, he can always repark the Bug off to the side so she can get out in the morning. He had a defiant impulse to stop off at Fogarty's but decided against it, not wanting to give her any more ammunition to use against him than she already has. By now, he is vaguely angry, resentful of the tone of her note. For a psychologist, he thinks, she doesn't know very much about people. It is at this moment that he grasps that something is wrong.

A strange man, wearing a three-piece suit and highly polished black leather pumps, is standing on Grote's back porch holding an envelope in his left hand. Maybe it is his wife's lover, come to confess and ask Grote's forgiveness. Before the man speaks, Grote realizes the true nature of his mission and his mind reels.

"Professor Grote?"

Timothy Grote nods.

"I'm Rob Dunstan, Mrs. Grote's attorney."

Grote nods again, wondering why they call themselves that, as if it makes earning a living off other people's private sorrow somehow nicer.

"Professor Grote, your wife is initiating divorce proceedings."

He stares blankly at the lawyer, wanting to ask why they'd done it this way instead of coming to his office. She could have at least given him a hint. Now he knows why she wanted him to come straight home.

"We didn't want to embarrass you on campus. You understand?"

Grote nods. Yes, he understands. The man hands him the envelope, which contains copies of the preliminary filing and a court order barring him from his house while his wife is present.

"That wasn't necessary," Grote says, breaking his silence. He notices the suitcase, the one she gave him for Christmas two years ago, standing off to the side, partially blocked by the balustrade.

"We'll arrange a convenient time this weekend for you to come and get your things. In the meantime, my advice to you is to consult with your own attorney. These matters are never pleasant, but perhaps we can work together to make this less unpleasant."

"Can I see my wife for a moment?"

"She prefers not to see you just now."

"Prefers not to. I see."

The man hands Grote his suitcase, signaling that the interview has ended. Grote wants to say something, to keep the conversation going and prolong, however futilely, some contact with the life that he has known and that is now drawing to a close. Above all, he wants desperately not to be disposable again.

"That's it?" he says. "Just like that?"

"I'm sorry," the lawyer says. "Believe me, it's easier this way."

As Grote jams his Volkswagen into reverse and backs out of his driveway, he is thinking that he'd like to hear the Four Tops again and stare at his lovely blue carpet with a beer in his hand and try to unravel the rug's mysteries. The lawyer is still standing on the back porch, and Grote's wife is nowhere to be seen, having finally passed, as per her wishes, out of his life.

He drives aimlessly around town, wondering where he'll spend the night, not wanting to knuckle under to the cliché by checking into a motel. Like a moth to a flame, he feels himself being drawn toward the Cork and Bottle, where he'll feel safe in the company of drinking companions. Undoubtedly, somebody will offer him a place to stay for tonight, and tomorrow he'll look for an apartment. With any luck, he'll be able to keep his stereo and the dead people's furniture.

A Grotean Quandary

At first, Professor Grote is perplexed by the dazzling display of postpubescent underpants in his American Literature 321 class. It begins the second Tuesday of the summer term: he's just finished reading aloud a particularly trenchant selection from Melville and is studying his students' faces for signs that something has registered on their consciousnesses. When his glance falls on Becky Petrowski, sophomore member of the cheerleading squad, she squirms in her seat and before anybody can do anything about it reveals to her awed instructor an astonishing expanse of pale blue nylon. Grote averts his eyes and begins shuffling his note cards nervously.

"Melville," he says self-consciously, "poses a question that is deeply rooted in Judeo-Christian tradition. Can anybody tell me what it is?"

Profound silence as Grote once again scans their faces, trying to avoid looking at the Petrowski girl, no easy task inasmuch as her seat is directly across from him. He steals one quick peek in her direction and, sure enough, she's doing it again. Probably doesn't realize what's happening, Grote thinks; the way these tables are set up, it's easy enough to forget that people can see underneath them. He looks at his watch in an exaggerated way, then at his class with what he hopes is a baleful expression.

"Look," he says, "you've all paid for fifteen more minutes of American Literature today. We can talk about Bartleby or continue to stare at each other. What'll it be? You there, Higgins, what do *you* think?"

Barry Higgins, preposterously tanned vice-president

of one of the more celebrated campus fraternities, squints sullenly at his interrogator. "Didn't read it," he shamelessly announces.

"Very well, then," Grote says with just a hint of bitterness in his voice. "I've had enough of this. Tomorrow, be prepared to write about 'Bartleby the Scrivener.' Class dismissed."

Alone in his office, Grote ponders what to do. The problem is the room he's been assigned—the students sit in molded plastic chairs around the outside of a U-shaped configuration of library tables. Grote delivers his lectures seated at a smaller table placed at the open end of the U. The room is normally occupied by the Women's Resource Center and Assertiveness Training Seminar; however, inasmuch as it is summer term and the Women's Studies Department is offering only two sections, Grote's literature class has been scheduled to meet there. Pictures of assertive women cover the walls, and notices advertising women's events are tacked on the bulletin board. Each day, Grote has to erase the blackboard because the instructor of the class preceding his, a chinless blonde who was married to a CPA before she got religion, asserts herself by leaving curious inscriptions for him to decipher. One day he was greeted by the word MEN! scrawled in huge block letters.

Another time, he arrived late to discover his entire class milling around outside the closed classroom door. Grote opened it and cautiously peered inside. The lights had been dimmed and the molded plastic chairs now formed a circle inside the U, and each chair was occupied by a woman with a serene expression on her face, holding hands with the woman on either side.

"What's this all about?" Grote had time to say before Ms. Rafferty made a rush at him and shooed him back out into the hallway.

"You've *ruined* it," she said in a vaguely bruised tone. "They were *feeling* it, getting in touch with their sisterhood."

"Well, it's 9:35," clever Grote said, performing for his students, who regarded the two professors as if they were exotic plants, "and *we're* supposed to be getting in touch with Jonathan Edwards."

"You can wait," Ms. Rafferty said. "This is important to their wellness. They've been assigned to assert themselves at home tonight and they require preparation and mutual support."

How would they do it? Grote pictured a husband, a lawyer perhaps, trudging home after a long day at work, wanting nothing more than a good stiff drink before dinner. To his utter amazement, his wife, who only that morning seemed perfectly sane, confronts him angrily and tells him to cook his own goddamned supper. What would the poor man do?

"This is what you teach in college?" he said.

Ms. Rafferty crossed her arms and glowered fiercely at him and didn't answer. If one disregarded her disappointing chin, Ms. Rafferty wasn't a bad-looking woman. Grote imagined himself standing behind her, hands resting lightly on her shoulders as he nibbled gently at her earlobe, arousing riotous passions in her until she could stand it no longer, whereupon they would throw off their clothes and leap into bed, giggling like schoolchildren. How would she like *that*?

"You've taken ten minutes of my class time," he said gruffly. "If you don't get those people out of there, I'm going to do it myself."

Ms. Rafferty turned on her heel and stomped back into the classroom.

Next morning, there was a memo in his mailbox from the dean reminding him that he was a guest of the Women's Studies Department and admonishing him to be "more tolerant of the non-traditional approaches to the important support systems we provide for the entire community."

The library tables have a surprising effect on Grote's students. Above the plane of the table tops, they are fairly attentive and well-mannered; beneath the surface, however, below the tables, Grote can sense seething unrest. Fidgeting, twitching, scratching themselves in inappropriate places, his students seem on the verge of open revolt. And they apparently think nobody can see what they're doing. Do they never look across the room and peep under the table? If they did and saw what their colleagues were doing, Grote is certain there would be an immediate change in classroom decorum.

He remembers pumping gas at the Shell station, one of his *ad hoc* careers as an undergraduate, and being endlessly amazed that people apparently didn't realize that he could see into their cars as he washed the windshields. His face no more than a foot and a half away while he solemnly scrubbed dead bugs off the glass, Grote watched people do extraordinary things, from smacking kids in the back seat to picking their noses to groping at each other in the front seat. And all as if he weren't even there.

As for Miss Petrowski, Grote has devised a plan. Before going home, he sneaks down the two flights of stairs to the Women's Studies Department and darts into his classroom. He removes a plastic chair from the stack in the corner and places it on the inside of the open rectangle directly across the table from where the Petrowski girl sits so that, should she be overcome by a desire to air out the insides of her thighs, she'll be shielded from unwelcome stares.

Wearing a new navy-blue bathing suit, Grote stands before the mirror in his bedroom, examining himself from as many angles as possible, alternately pulling in his stomach and letting it droop, generally pleased with what he sees. True, there is some fat around his middle, but what the heck, he thinks, he's forty-three and still in pretty good shape. Since his wife left six years ago, Grote has become increasingly vain about his appearance, as if to compensate for the part of his self-esteem that she took with her. He dresses more casually now and is fond of wearing brightly colored knit shirts, blue jeans, and loafers, particularly during the summer term when everything is casual. Not that he'll ever go as far as that Thwacker fellow in Psychology, who lectures in tennis shorts.

"Not bad, Grotey, not bad at all," he says, slapping himself on the belly, then reaching for an orange T-shirt on the dresser.

Determined that his students will repent of their indolence, Grote works on preparing their quiz but is unable to shake the image of Becky Petrowski, which flashes before him continually, ruining his concentration. She is a pretty little thing, he has to admit. Suppose she fancies him, he muses, then immediately censures himself. She's a mere girl, young enough to be his daughter. It had to be an accident; she couldn't have any idea what she was doing. Still, the vision of that patch of blue cloth and those glistening thighs won't go away.

Ms. Rafferty has been hard at work by the time Grote arrives for class, quiz in hand, the next morning. He spots her as she's leaving the room, wearing bright red shorts, a white oxford-cloth blouse, and high-heeled sandals that lace around her ankles, and looking, he thinks, more like a member of the Junior League than a sexual revolutionary. She gives him a sort of half smile, which he interprets as a subtle payback for some injustice inflicted on the female race by the likes of him. She has incredibly long legs and he wonders why he never noticed before. Then again, she didn't arrive until January (hired to fill in for Ms. Whyme, who was sent off to Baltimore on an administrative internship and who will no doubt return in a year or so to wreak havoc from the dean's office). Grote has an impulse to say something witty to Ms. Rafferty, but keeps his mouth shut.

MEN *NEED* WOMEN; WOMEN, HOWEVER, CAN SURVIVE
WITHOUT MEN

"Balderdash," grumbles Grote as he begins erasing the board. The trap he set for Miss Petrowski is intact, but she foils him by sitting one seat over and languorously draping her left leg on the chair intended to protect her while her right leg remains at an oblique angle, proclaiming to anybody who cares to look at the gap in her cheerleading shorts that her underwear drawer has yielded up yellow today. "Hmph," snorts Grote.

As his students are laboring over their quiz (single question: What does Herman Melville imply is the answer to the age-old question "Am I my brother's keeper?") Grote busies himself with tomorrow's lecture on Edgar Allan Poe. Fifteen minutes into the hour, he idly scans the room and discovers a remarkable thing: a veritable plague of underwear. Three seats to Miss Petrowski's left, Penny Krieger is displaying lime green; next to her, homely Nancy Starkey is flashing red; across from them, to Grote's left, blond Sheri Greene exhibits sensible white cotton. More disconcerting is the fact that the boys are doing it too. Barry Higgins and two of his cohorts, all wearing identical unlaced running shoes, black tennis shorts, lavender T-shirts, and fraternity baseball caps, hunch like gnomes over their quiz papers with their legs set in identical straddles under the table, telltale bulges all over the place. Grote rises and leaves the room, suddenly overcome by a need for a drink of water.

Bent far over the drinking fountain, mouth almost touching the spigot, Grote slurps the tepid water, which, owing to low pressure, burbles out weakly. Behind him, he hears the clicking of high heels on the terrazzo floor. Ms. Rafferty! he thinks, just as a surge of pressure splashes water in his face and on his neck and shirt.

"Aren't you supposed to be teaching?"

"They're taking a quiz," Grote says, wiping his face and neck with his handkerchief.

"Hmm," Ms. Rafferty says, as if what Grote has said is vaguely distasteful.

"Yes," Grote says, nodding his head and feeling ridiculous. "There's something strange going on in there."

"Somehow that doesn't surprise me," Ms. Rafferty

says, terminating the interview abruptly by turning away from him and click-click-clicking her way down the hall, her blond hair swaying rhythmically. Grote watches until she turns into an adjacent hallway, entertaining lascivious thoughts, which he quickly cancels. No way, he thinks.

Back in the classroom, Grote leans forward with his head tipped down, as if poring over the textbook, simultaneously avoiding looking at his students and preventing them from noticing the wet spot on the front of his shirt. Higgins and company are the last to leave, handing in nearly blank papers.

"What did you *do* all hour?" Grote says, shaking his head.

"Oh, the usual," Higgins says, and the three dissolve into unbecoming giggles, leading Grote to suspect them of taking drugs.

When they are gone, Grote attacks the pile of chairs in the corner and doesn't quit until he's erected a solid wall around the inside of the rectangle, determined that this foolishness must stop if he is to have any success this summer. Like it or not, those students will know something about American literature by the middle of August, and they're not going to learn anything by staring across the room at each other's crotches.

Next morning, Ms. Rafferty, attired in white shorts, a navy-blue blouse, and a white headband, frowns at him sternly. Inside, the protective wall is gone and all the extra chairs are stacked in the corner again. Ms. Rafferty has left him a message:

POLITE GUESTS DO NOT REARRANGE THE FURNITURE

"Damn it, Ms. Rafferty," Grote mutters as he's erasing the board. He places the lectern, which he doesn't normally use, on the table and delivers his lecture standing, his right leg propped on the chair he usually sits in, figuring that his students will be more attentive if they have to focus up and toward the front of the room. Moreover, when he's standing, Grote can't see under the tables, and he doesn't want to know what's going on there. His vexation with Ms. Rafferty builds during the hour, occasionally distracting him from his lecture. Who does that woman think she is?

It is worth noting that Timothy Grote has not always been a purveyor of literary tradition. At one time in his life, albeit against his will, he was a soldier and has been in a war, an experience that altered his outlook considerably. He loathes groups, despises all -*isms* except humanism (he's even beginning to wonder about that), and thinks psychology is a swindle. At faculty meetings (which he generally refuses to attend) he can be counted on to vote against the majority and nearly always says something outrageous at least once during each seance. His colleagues tolerate his eccentricity with jovial good humor, in large measure because they do not understand its source.

Being at war makes anything else seem trivial. Sitting in a bunker with a machine gun in his lap, senses stretched taut, wary, expectant, above all *ready* for something, had a profound effect on Grote. Afterwards, he felt he'd never been as totally alive in his life as during those moments of absolute tension. Now, he disdains academic politics as petty, sordid squabbles, and has little regard for anyone who takes such things seriously. Whether Grote is correct is both uncertain and irrelevant; what is certain is that such iconoclasm, if known, would not endear him to his fellow pedants.

What Grote believes in is literature and the primacy of the human imagination, next to which, in his view, the very cosmos seems puny. His colleagues, each of whom has staked out his plot in the kingdom of literature—the open meadow of romanticism, the swamp of naturalism, and north forty of Shakespeare—seem content in their own precincts and uninterested in their neighbors' affairs. Grote sometimes worries that they don't love literature anymore. They, in turn, regard him as a harmless dayhiker and forgive his occasional trespasses on their turf.

None of which alters the fact that something must

be done about his students flashing their underwear while he's trying to lecture.

"Just what the *hell* do you think you're doing in *my* classroom?" Ms. Rafferty towers in the doorway to Grote's office, feet planted firmly, hands defiantly resting on nicely rounded hips, in a confrontation mode, probably acquired at an assertiveness seminar. Grote, sitting in his swivel chair, is at a definite disadvantage, but he remains where he is. Were he to stand, hostilities would likely escalate.

"Calm down, Ms. Rafferty. I can explain everything."

"Hmph," says Ms. Rafferty. "There's nothing to explain. You barge into my territory uninvited and then try to take over. I won't have it. If this doesn't stop immediately, the dean will hear of it."

"You're going to tattle on me again?"

Ms. Rafferty emits a guttural, growling sound and fixes Grote with a menacing gaze. It occurs to him that he's dead wrong if he thinks he can explain anything to this sexual warrior-politician.

"You're just like all men," Ms. Rafferty hisses. "You're only happy when you're . . ."

Grote raises his hand in a STOP! gesture. "Don't waste your breath, Ms. Rafferty. I had a reason for placing the chairs as I did, and I assure you that it had nothing to do with you. I'll try to think of another solution to my problem."

Ms. Rafferty, jaw tightly set, glares at him for a full ten seconds, shakes her head disgustedly, then is gone.

So much anger, Grote thinks sadly, bottled up inside that woman. Rumor has it that her former husband had to cough up quite a lot of loot when they were divorced. He can't understand her resentment, particularly if, as rumor again has it, it was she who divorced him. That crack about him being like all men annoys him; such generalizations are dangerous. Ms. Rafferty is not an unattractive woman. Under different circumstances, Grote reflects, they could have become friends, and then who knows what miracles might have happened. Too bad it turned out like this, but that's the way things are. Grote places Ms. Rafferty on a back shelf in his mental storeroom.

As for his American Literature 321 class, Grote supposes he can finish the term lecturing the way he did this morning. As long as his students behave themselves on the surface, what goes on under the tables is no concern of his. If they don't read their assignments, there will be more quizzes, and with luck, they will have learned something by the end of the term. Then, Grote will take a nice trip, to the Catskills perhaps, where he will undoubtedly ponder the relationship between politics and literature.

Grote Discovers Himself Trapped in Time

IT is Saturday when Grote's sister calls with the stunning news.

Ordinarily, Grote would rather go to the dentist or undergo a prostate examination than talk to his sister, who bores him with interminable, trivial crises, most recently the imponderable dilemma of whether the new subcompact station wagon she and her husband, Jimmy, were about to purchase should be light gray or dark blue (they settled on canary yellow). Once, when he was in the Army, he almost got into trouble over one of her emergency calls having to do with something their father said to their mother in a restaurant. This time, however, she's really on to something.

"Not Irish, you say?"

"She was born in Scotland, just across the border from Newcastle."

"I suppose that would explain how she met great-grandfather Grote."

"And get this: in 1916, in Steubenville, Ohio, Grampa was *divorced*."

"Well, the old rascal," Grote says.

"That makes Grandma his *second wife*."

"No kidding."

"It's not *funny*, Timothy. What are we going to *do* about it?"

She's on a roll now, and he allows her to rattle on, interjecting an occasional "Hm," "Uh huh," or "Really?" This particular quandary is absolutely perfect, as it can never be resolved: Grote's grandfather died in 1958, his grandmother ten years later. In his

mind's eye, Grote sees his grandfather in the leather-
covered rocker on his front porch: small, wizened,
surprisingly barrel-chested, with white hair, octagonal
metal-rimmed bifocals, and large, deep-lobed ears
("Like a taxicab with the doors open," Grote can actually hear his grandfather's voice). Dawdling over his
vision, he sees himself in miniature, a four-year-old
Grote, arms over his head, struggling to push his grandfather's old lawnmower while the old man pares his
fingernails with a pearl-handled pocketknife. Afterwards, his grandfather would come down to help, then
they'd walk to the dairy a block and a half away for ice
cream. In Grote's imagination it is 1949, and he can
smell the freshly cut grass, bask in the steamy Michigan heat, hear his grandfather's laughter: everything is
as it was.

"I mean, *nobody* got divorced in 1916," his sister
interrupts his reverie. "It's almost sordid when you
think about it."

"Nonsense," Grote replies. "Grandfathers have to
have fun, too. Besides, if he didn't, none of us would be
here to talk about it."

This bit of impeccable logic, which Grote supposes
will stop her dead in her tracks, doesn't affect her at
all. It seems that his sister, who spirited away a mysterious wooden cigar box moments after his grandmother died, has just now gotten around to looking
inside. From a distance of a thousand miles, she cata-
logs its contents in somber, pious tones: birth certi-
ficates galore, including the aforementioned great-
grandmother's; his grandfather's divorce decree; the
deed to a house that was torn down in 1934; cracked
photographs of people his sister can't identify; newspaper clippings: LOCAL MAN [Grote's father] WOUNDED
IN FRANCE; the keys to one of his grandfather's Stude-
bakers; other treasures.

"Interesting," says Grote. "Why don't you box
everything up and send it here so I can have a look
at it?"

"When will I get it back?" challenges his sly sister.

Now that she's uncovered this mystery, she intends to
hang onto the loot.

"Jesus Christ," he says impatiently, "you've had
that stuff nearly twenty years."

"You don't have to swear," she sulks.

"Then send copies."

"I can't do it right now because of Angie's wedding
on Saturday."

(Who the hell is Angie, Grote wonders.)

Toward the end of the conversation, his sister makes
her usual pitch for him to visit them in Michigan, and
he declines politely, as usual. The last time he saw
them was at his brother's funeral, eight years ago. For
a while, it seemed, Grotes were dropping like flies:
there had been unpleasantness about his mother's and
great-aunt Martha's estates, and there was unpleasantness about his brother, as well. Grote's not ready to
visit, though he's been in Michigan several times without telling anybody.

The Tigers are playing in Kansas City, and Grote turns
on his black-and-white television at one o'clock, in-
tending to while away the afternoon drinking beer and
watching the ball game. He's got a batch of papers to
grade but has already decided they can wait until tomorrow. His floppy-eared grandfather, dead nearly
thirty years now, has risen in his estimation: it was
undoubtedly quite an accomplishment to get divorced
in 1916. Grote is certain that his sister won't send that
copy of the decree, so he'll never know for sure what it
was all about. Probably adultery, he decides, unable to
imagine any other grounds for divorce in those days.
He speculates awhile on who might have done what to
whom, then dismisses it as irrelevant.

Detroit is sloppy today, fumbling with the ball in
the outfield and missing throws to the cutoff men.
Grote remembers his grandmother, the dour Christian
Scientist, solemnly keeping Tiger box scores, as if it
were a religious devotion. She would sit by the radio,
and later in front of the television, holding a grudge

against the entire city of Cleveland because of something the Indians did to the Tigers in 1948. After she died, they found hundreds of her box scores in the drawer of the china closet, her neat, crimped handwriting preserving, on the backs of envelopes and scraps of paper, the feats of ballplayers who'd long since retired, many of them dead. What would she have thought about his grandfather's divorce?

As far as Grote knew as a child, all grandparents slept in separate rooms. He attributed this to his grandmother's being a Christian Scientist, temperance advocate, and former suffragette, while his grandfather was Episcopalian and prone to extemporaneous drinking, particularly when he went fishing, which Grote's grandmother sanctioned in order to get the old man out of her hair. When Grote got older, he merely assumed that at some point his grandmother had decided that his grandfather's nocturnal companionship was something she could live without. This divorce business adds a new wrinkle, however.

Suppose she didn't find out about it until after they were married? He pictures his grandmother as a nervous virgin, having been warned by her gorgon of a mother that something dreadful will happen after the wedding ceremony, when she and her husband are alone. (As he's seen plenty of photographs of the principals, this is easy for Grote.) However, instead of the expected dreadful thing, her new husband sits next to her on the edge of the bridal bed and announces sheepishly that this isn't the first time for him, and that she is in fact the second Mrs. Grote. Rubbish, thinks Grote, his grandfather wouldn't have been such a rat as that. There are other possibilities.

The probability that his grandfather, enthralled by passion for Esther Seidl, divorced the other woman in order to marry her is so remote that Grote doesn't consider it at all, except to dismiss it. He never knew his grandfather to be passionate about anything other than Harry Truman, whom he detested (the only blot, as far as Grote can tell, on the old man's character). Besides, the divorce was in 1916, and his grandparents didn't get married until after the Armistice; had they been in a frenzy, they wouldn't have waited so long. Far more likely that his grandfather, scandalized in Steubenville, left town to avoid the gossip that would have accompanied his indiscretion. Seventy years after the fact, Grote experiences pangs of clemency for his grandfather and scorn for the people who drove him out of town, all of whom must be dead by now.

"Gentlemen of the jury," Grote addresses his television, "these are the facts as they are known to us: in 1916, at the age of thirty-two, John Grote either divorced or was divorced by a woman about whom we know nothing. This occurred in Steubenville, Ohio, and we do not know what issues were involved in this divorce, nor do we know of any issue involved.

"We do know that John Grote married Esther Seidl in Utica, Michigan, shortly after the Armistice, also that her parents, Bavarian immigrants, distrusted the short Englishman with big ears. Moreover, Esther and her sister, Martha, became Christian Scientists and suffragettes shortly before passage of the Nineteenth Amendment, further that this occurred after Esther's marriage to John Grote.

"The Grotes' only child, John, Jr., born in 1920, seems to have inherited his mother's severe outlook as well as his father's predisposition to alcohol, in consequence of which his liver blew out in 1970. (RIP John Grote, Jr.) Sometime between the conception of their son and 1948, when their grandson Timothy was big enough to be poking around on his own, Esther and John Grote began sleeping apart.

"These are the facts. Gentlemen, what say you?"

The verdict is unanimous: John Grote would have told his bride-to-be of his previous marriage, thereby making the Steubenville affair irrelevant to the matter of where he and his wife slept between 1920 and 1948. The Seidl girls were strong-willed, inasmuch as suffragettes and members of a matriarchal religion could hardly have been otherwise. In marrying Esther Seidl, John Grote came between the sisters; they, in turn, asserted their wills in the manner previously indicated. Bored with sex and tired of her husband's incessant snoring (Grote can vouch for the snoring), Esther moved out of John's bed around 1930. Had it not been for her ten-year-old son and the fact that the Depression was hard upon them, she might have handed John Grote his second defeat in as many outings.

DIAGNOSIS: Unindicated Feminism
FINAL SCORE: Detroit 7, Kansas City 3

Grote sips from a can of beer while listening to Wagnerian overtures on KFRZ. He doesn't particularly approve of Wagner but has no choice if he wants to listen to classical music; KPQR, the other public station, is playing progressive jazz just now. Grote marvels at his existence, at the fact that he can approve or disapprove of things, can take pleasure in the Tigers' victory, enjoy the taste of the Budweiser as it slides easily down his throat.

An infinite number of things had to happen exactly as they did in order for Grote to exist, and the odds against him sitting in his chair with a can of beer in his hand are enormous. Had his grandfather not been divorced in 1916; had his grandparents selected a day other than the one they chose for their amours; had his grandmother, in turning on her side afterwards, squished the semen inside her in a slightly different way, allowing a different sperm cell to reach her egg, Grote's father would not have been born. Grote sighs; without his father, there could be no Grote. Likewise in the case of his mother and her parents and grandparents, all the way back, back, and back, even before the time when slithery antecedents cowered in primeval forests.

More recently, when Roman legions marauded in Britain, who was favored or not favored, murdered or not murdered, raped or not raped that Grote might sip

his beer in smug satisfaction over the results of a baseball game? Who did the Danes, William the Con-
queror, or Oliver Cromwell spare that Grote might
live? Grote wonders about these things and I wonder,
too. For answers, the closest Grote can get is a tattered
divorce decree that he will more than likely never get
to look at, and what scant information it might supply
will be useful only insofar as it explains things that
didn't happen. The rest is lost forever. Grote feels pro-
foundly isolated from those irretrievably trapped in
time and whose genes he carries.

Supposing he could conjure them up, what would
they talk about? "Hey, Great-great-great-great-great-
uncle Rolf—how's it going, big fella? Say, I've been
meaning to ask you how things were during the Nor-
man Conquest. Lots of pillaging and stuff like that,
huh?" Impossible scenario, Grote admits, if for no
other reason than Uncle Rolf wouldn't understand a
word he was saying and would probably smack him a
good one with his quarterstaff.

His last real opportunity to delve into his pedigree
came when his great-aunt Martha, seventy-eight and
already a trifle dotty, was laid up in the hospital with a
broken hip. All he could get out of her was a meander-
ing account of a buggy ride she and her sister, Esther,
took to Romeo, Michigan, in 1902 to have their photographs taken together, wearing ribbons that had been
ordered from Detroit specially for the occasion. (Grote
has one of the photos even now, in a tarnished gilt
frame on his mantel.) After that, she lapsed into a brief
slumber, waking with a start and mistaking Grote for
his father.

"It's a sin to swear, but damn you, Johnny Grote!"
she shrieked. "You're a disgrace to your family with
that alcohol."

"Aunt Martha, it's me, Tim," Grote said gently.
"Johnny's gone; he died two years ago."

"Don't talk back. You're a bum, Johnny, and if you
think you're getting one cent from me you've got another think coming."

A nurse entered and told Grote to clear out because she'd been doing that for the past ten days, heaping maledictions on Grote's father every day after her naps. Whenever he went back, the same thing happened. In the end, they told him not to visit his aunt anymore because it upset her too much. Grote's sister went instead. He never knew what went on between them, but when the woman died they found that she'd changed her will, leaving the bulk of her estate to charities.

Not that Grote cares a fig about genealogy, the dreary province of gimcrack notability. Who and what those people were in the dim recesses of the past doesn't inspire in him anything more than idle curiosity. Rather, more personally and selfishly, he marvels that he has evolved from their having lived and reproduced. In this vain conception, he imagines all the Grote progenitors, their lives an unending series of meanness and want, toiling away in solemn foolery so that their line might spawn, generations down the pike, Timothy Grote, unremarkable assistant professor of literature at a third-rate university. Preposterous doctrine!

Having dispensed with that, Grote has another notion. Language is failing him, but he is aware of feelings and attitudes that infuse his existence, not with hope, necessarily, but with a sense of credibility, perhaps. He likes being alive: the planet, shabby, truculent, and fraught with ideology, suits him well enough. He feels remarkably fortunate to be able to watch baseball games, drink beer, and teach literature at a third-rate university. Seen in this light, the nameless, indispensable ancestors attain a new significance, and Grote experiences a twinge of gratitude for their having lived and passed on, however dispassionately, the genetic wherewithal to make his existence possible. In fact, it occurs to him that, for the first time in his life, he is truly grateful to be alive. He would like to be able to thank somebody, but there's nobody left to thank. Grote feels singular, isolated, unexampled, and damned happy to be breathing.

Now that that's settled, there remains that business about Great-grandmother Grote, nee McMahon. That's really something—Grote has lived half his life under the false impression that he's one-eighth Irish. The Potato Famine and Easter Uprising of 1916 (the coincidence of this being also the year of his grandfather's divorce does not go unnoticed by Grote) have had significance for him. Faced with new truth, our bogus Irishman must make adjustments. No longer can he contemplate the massacres at Drogheda and Wexford with anything other than detached, academic interest; nor can he continue to harbor the same personal grudge against Oliver Cromwell. Parnell, De Valera, and O'Connell, names he has celebrated over foaming pints of Guinness at the Irish-American Club in Detroit, must be assigned new places in Grote's mental pantheon. Joyce, Swift, and Shaw are no longer his countrymen.

"Not Irish," he says. "I'll be damned."

Now that he's Scottish, alterations must be made, and he knows it will be some time before the metamorphosis becomes apparent. Already, though, he is beginning to feel sympathetic stirrings for Mary, Queen of Scots. Edward the Second undoubtedly got what he had coming to him at Bannockburn. First thing in the morning, Grote decides, he's going to the library to read up on the Glencoe massacre to find out what that scoundrel William of Orange did to his people in 1692. Already, he can feel his indignation rising. Grote reckons he's going to like being Scottish.